Performances of a

# DEATH METAL BARD

*A Brutal Novella*

# ROB LEIGH

LEIGH BOOKS



eBook ISBN: 979-8-9888734-4-0
Paperback ISBN: 979-8-9888734-3-3
Book Cover Art by Daly Chochon
First edition 2024

# SETLIST

This book is dedicated to anyone who ever
played music for their friends and were
asked "You like this?"

Hell yeah we do
and you might too.

Listen to the songs that inspired me to
write this novella:

# Smoke & Mirrors

# Smoke & Mirrors

T hey say that some things never get old, but when it came to starving, I had to disagree.

A grumbling, whining stomach that pawed at my innards like a dog was as annoying as it was worrying. *I knew* I was hungry. I could have done without the reminders. Nothing to do about it but offer a shrug and a sigh, the same as I'd been doing for months now.

A jolt in the cart robbed me of my balance, sending my forehead plowing into the wooden crate brimming with cheaply made, scratchy textiles. A loose stitch caught me just above the brow and carved a lengthy score diagonally across my forehead. Brutal.

A trickle of moisture dribbled down my face and I wiped away the inky blood. The fading corpsepaint on my brow smeared with the ichor. *Can't this damned idiot drive?* I looked back at what the cart had hit. A lone rock jutted above the dirt of the country road, the *only* object in sight and entirely avoidable. The driver, a scruffy merchant, snickered loudly. Perhaps the trader just wanted to see if I did in fact bleed or if I was as bloodless as my face paint made me look. But I did, just as much as any other elf.

"There was a rock," I mumbled. I received a short grunt in reply.

Rapidly slingshotting past middle age, the merchant's rum-stained wool cap was tightly gripped to a patchy head of peppery hair. A beard grown extensively for the purpose of hiding a weak chin did an equally poor job of hiding his smirk.

I blotted my brow again with my raggedy sleeve and squinted ahead to the tree line at the end of the bend in the road. Farmland and recently planted crops rose over hills to both sides and behind me. Maybe that was the cause of my sneezing yesterday. My new lute jostled in the pile of textiles and clattered to the bottom of the cart with an out-of-tune twang. *New* was a misnomer as the piece of junk looked ancient. But after my old one had broken during a tavern brawl that I hadn't even started, this was the best that I could do. Barely worth cheating in cards over, but it was mine now.

The trees ahead grew larger to reveal a dense wood on either side of the road. Blessed shade, after days of nothing but sun, was just beyond.

And hopefully opportunity within that shade. My stomach constricted again with a tedious gurgle. I surely would find more here than anywhere else I had searched. The highway patrol outpost hadn't been in need of a bard, much less one that plays Death Metal. The monastery didn't pay, it turned out, and you had to be religious to get their food. The carnival went up in flames two days after I had been hired, and I was surprised it had lasted as long as it did. It was poor practice to give goblins sole creative control of the fireworks. Nothing but misfortune everywhere I turned.

"*Murder*," the voice rasped.

And atop the usual messes, I was going mad.

At least, it felt that way. A few days after I'd won the lute it had started talking to me, and so far only I could hear it. I stole a furtive glance at the instrument, fearing that resting my eyes upon it would elicit more one or two-word sentences about murder. The damn thing would never stay in tune either. The merchant hadn't noticed it yet. Either he was too thick to register the voice or humans really were as numb to magic as I'd heard.

I examined the merchant's map, turning it one way and another, trying to pinpoint the distance to our destination. "Is that forest up ahead where this town is? Moshanda?"

"It's *Moashanda*," the man grumbled through his teeth and a swig of rum. "Freak."

"Right," I bit my lip. The next stop on my tour of potential employment opportunities, Moashanda was said to have a great deal of local folk, and that meant at least a tavern or two in need of entertainment. Maybe even *my* kind of entertainment.

My particular brand of music was not what many would call popular, especially since I had invented it. The grumbling, harsh growls of my voice always contrasted with the lighter tone of my instrument, and it created a garbled mess that never seemed to land with an audience. No instrument I'd found had produced the sound I sought and I doubted one ever would. I wouldn't compromise and play something else either. Life never felt more interesting or full than with a thunderous, razor-sharp riff in my ears, even if it was just wistful imagination.

*"Find him."*

I shot a worried glance at the Lute. "That's new," I muttered.

The scored and scratched wood of the Lute was painted over with a blood-red stain, a color I had never seen for any instrument. Strings stripped down so thin they might snap any second, a gash in the back of the neck, several missing pegs from the pegbox. It certainly *looked* like it had seen a murder or two.

As we approached and eventually passed the tree line, I set to gathering my things. I began by pulling on and lacing my hole-ridden, charcoal-covered boots. I ended by checking my pockets for the canvas coin pouch. The trader glanced back from the front of the cart, keenly interested in the coin that I had promised him.

Moashanda came into view over the next hour through the tree line. The only stop on a traveler's journey through this forest, it was a rapidly growing town on its way to becoming a city. Plentiful wood and a river nearby, I couldn't imagine a reason someone wouldn't want to settle down here. Quaint, sturdy cottages were dotted throughout well-constructed town blocks. Limestones lined the edges of the road, and the bustling of the main square could be heard from outside of town. The steeple of a temple marked the very center of the settlement.

Our cart reached the outermost circle of the town, and a trading post beckoned to the left. Some of the market traders, a mix of elves and humans, didn't look very enthusiastic about my escort or his trading stock, but those grimaces could very well have been directed at me.

"Bringing more than just furs and textiles today, eh Borgen?" one of the traders shouted.

Apparently answering to the name of Borgen, the merchant driving my cart grunted, "Aye, chartered me for passage back near Galmin. Figured he couldn't stiff me any worse than you lot do." He laughed a bit too hard at a joke that he must have been working on the whole duration of our four-day ride. His laugh bounced back as irked chuckles from the others.

I looked down at my tightly laced boots.

"Well, better be on your way soon, stranger," the marketeer called. "This town has enough troubles without some outsider wandering around and stirring things up." I bit my tongue harder than I expected. Nothing friendly existed behind his voice.

Borgen dismounted the cart and gave the lone horse pulling it a congratulatory pat. "Deal is a deal, I got you here to Moashanda. Now my fee." But when he looked back to the cart, I was already sprinting away, Lute in hand.

Dirt scraped my feet through the holes in my boots, and the spray of pebbles after each step accompanied the fading shouts of Borgen and the other traders. My black, tattered coat streamed behind me as I ran into the bustling town. Even if I had bothered to fasten the one button the thing had left, it wouldn't have held.

"Stop him! That freak stole from me!" Borgen shouted. I rolled my eyes against the wind in my face. As if he had anything worth taking. I'd simply hitched a ride on his wagon.

The problem was that his shouting worked. Several townsfolk, a mixture of humans, goblins, and even some elves, whipped their gazes in my direction, eyes narrowed with suspicion. My appearance certainly didn't give the impression of an upstanding citizen.

*So I can't run this way.* I turned and darted down another street, away from the busy center of the settlement. These roads were much less populated, and a much better option. Passersby followed me with confused stares, eyebrows furrowing into bows at the sight of a face-painted newcomer tearing through their street with three winded merchants hollering after him. Thankfully, none found me worth pursuing on my run to the hills.

After several turns and getting myself thoroughly lost, I found myself panting, hands on my knees and doubled over, at another edge of town. Which edge, I wasn't quite sure. I decided it was a problem for when I caught my breath.

I panted and swiped my hair back behind my ears, wishing the tapered points held it out of my face better than a tie would have. My left pant leg was an inch or two shorter than the right from where I had torn a strip off the garment last week—a rudimentary hair tie at best that fell out immediately. The Lute sat in the dirt where I had carefully set it. It may have been in terrible condition, but it was the only instrument I had now, and therefore needed my respect.

"*Find him. Murder,*" the Lute buzzed.

"Shut up," I mumbled.

I pulled the canvas coin pouch from my coat pocket and undid the drawstring around the top. When I poured the pebbles from the pouch and onto the ground, I had to admit that it didn't sound anything like actual coins. Borgen had been especially gullible, and there was no guarantee I would be lucky enough to find such an easy mark again.

I wiped my hands on my pant legs and stood, plucking the Lute up by the neck. Now to find a way to get some *actual* coin. The commotion that I'd caused when coming into town would definitely make that harder. I cursed myself for being so stupid. At any point before we pulled up to town, I could have run into the woods and then snuck into town without Borgen seeing.

"And that's why you're starving," I scolded myself. My stomach chimed in with an accusing growl. I grumbled back at my gut and set off back into town. The sun was sinking over the tree line, meaning that dusk in town would come much quicker than it would outside these towering pines.

Moashanda didn't seem as vibrant as it had from the outside. Sure, townsfolk walked the streets, but with a much more watchful disposition than I had noticed before. Coin purses were clutched tightly along with a few visible weapons, parents reigned their children in close, and groups of villagers maintained a healthy distance from each other. Village aldermen prowled the streets with swords ready to unsheathe. High crime rate in a place like this? The scene I'd caused when I arrived wouldn't have been enough for everyone in town—mostly humans with a few noticeable Elves—to be this paranoid. It was times like this that I wished my coat had a cowl attached, but that cost money. I didn't have a very stable relationship with money.

Staying in what shadows were available in the late afternoon sun, I skirted most big groups and surveyed my employment options.

I waded into a much louder sea of murmurs as the market spread out before me. This must have been just outside the center of town, for the temple's shadow leaned over the market square like an instructor peering at an apprentice's calligraphy over their shoulder. Scents of spiced goods wafted from a trio of tents off to the left. A duo of brewers peddled their "authentically original" ale that looked and smelled suspiciously familiar. Trinkets and treasures filled every table, stand, and shelf.

A raucous sludge of laughter, shouting, beverages sluicing on the ground, and some drunken tears made my ears perk up. The unmistakable symphony of a tavern always spelled an opportunity to perform, and a wide grin overtook my face. A few passersby flinched and gave me a wide berth at the sight of my smile. A typical response from most who saw me. I'd had no choice but to get used to it over the years, but it still stung.

"*Alone*," the Lute said.

My feet carried me toward the large but shoddy alehouse before my nerves could convince me not to. At the very least, it would get me sufficiently drunk to forget how hungry I was. Another gurgle from my stomach indicated it would keep reminding me. Alcohol-soaked mud gushed into my holey boots, chilling my toes with gritty sludge.

Twelve or so feet from the heavy, wooden doors, a fist whistled toward my face from the aether beyond my vision to the right. I barely ducked before the fist smashed into its intended target: the face of a pudgy, brown-haired man that had been standing on my left. The local drunks grappled with each other, hiccupping through their growled curses.

"I saw you stealing my sheep last night, thief!" the man who'd done the punching said.

"You have more than enough, you didn't need all of 'em," the bruising man shot back.

Everyone in the surrounding crowd, including the man who'd done the punching, looked shocked at the confession. It was as if they had expected him to refute it.

"You low-living heap o' filth! I ought to gut you in the street here. What happened to the man that helped me build my stable, eh?"

The brown-haired sheep thief shook his head, "I don't know what you're on about, but if it's a fight you want, I'll share one with you!"

I sidestepped the brawl and paced carefully up the cracking stone steps. The doors looked much older than the rest of the building. The dark wood suggested layer upon layer of lacquer and stain. New planks of varying color made up the rest of the structure, suggesting that the place had endured several fires throughout its existence. An old but ornately carved sign with several scorch marks hung above the doors, bearing the words *The Piper King's Pit*.

The cumbersome doors pushed open with some effort, and my eyes widened at the intense, warm, and smoky atmosphere that greeted me. Tables and chairs crammed every square inch of the main hall, a cavernous space with a vaulted ceiling. Wooden beams stretched high overhead, sporting banners of the kingdom's provinces. From the center beam hung a green and purple banner with a flute in the center. Around the neck of the flute sat a gold crown, a symbol of King Kevan. Apparently, the King of Enotia had been quite a renowned bard before stumbling into the throne.

Flagons of ale, cups of rum, whiskey, and other spiced spirits that I hadn't even heard of changed hands and flowed more fiercely than the nearby river. Whatever troubles this town had, many of its citizens obviously made a point to try and forget them here. There was still a tension in the air, but it was dampened by the blurry stupor that was being shitfaced.

On the way to the bar, I glimpsed two men sitting in a cleared area toward the back, warming up and tuning their fiddles. I grinned and kept going, hand tightly gripping my Lute. My booze-muddy boots squelched loudly with each step to the barkeep's counter.

Already, the tavern keeper was displeased to see me. "What do you want?" he growled. His wide brow had a cavernous crease, and his beady eyes sported permanent bags. Barkeep in this town must not have been a relaxing job of late.

"What's going on up there?" I asked, pointing toward the stage area.

"Contest of song," he rasped. "Winner takes home the prize."

"Which is?"

"Two hundred gold scales," he said. "Second place is one hundred."

"Metal. Sign me up," I said.

The man's eyes scrunched in confusion through his permanent scowl; my words were like a foreign language to him. "And what do you play?"

"Death Metal." I lifted my chin, trying to appear nonchalant. If I projected calm, perhaps he would find me endearing.

Instead, the barkeep started to lose his patience. He glanced at the patrons occupying the bar to either side of me, who I then noticed were no less than a head and a half taller than me.

"Please sign me up," I repeated, hefting my Lute. "This town looks like it could blow off some steam."

He looked me up and down before nodding slowly, "Fine, but if you start any trouble, you don't come back in my tavern. Hear me?"

An optimistic smile crept across my face. My grin made the man scowl further.

The man waved me away, and I sauntered off, letting my smile fully conquer my face despite my stomach insisting that the day wasn't won. I just needed to play a couple songs and hope someone liked it. Someone here had to connect with my music, right?

"Eh! What's your name? You'll be going fifth," the barman called.

"Ozzymandias," I shouted back.

"Oz-what?"

I rolled my eyes. "Just call me Mandy." I turned back toward the door.

*You still have to win, you know,* my stomach grumbled. *And you still don't have the sound you want. The lutes you've had before are all too purified. You need something raw and dark, not light and whimsical.*

It wasn't like I had much of a choice. No instruments made that kind of sound. A few absentminded picks of the worn strings on this new Lute confirmed that its out-of-tune twang was decidedly lacking in brutality.

I shook my head free of these troublesome thoughts. The most promising chance of gaining coin in months had just fallen into my lap, and it would not slip through my fingers. Just had to sit and tune this thing up, then play. Nothing else mattered.

I was two steps from the door when a burly hand clapped down on my shoulder. For a moment, I had to convince myself that it wasn't a tree stump with gnarled roots gripping my coat.

The hand was attached to one of the two men from the bar. His absolute block of a jaw was set somewhere between disgust and contempt. I'd seen this look many times before. Some poser wanted to show the outcast that he wasn't welcome here.

"Don't come back in here," Block-Jaw spat.

I tried on my most polite smile, "Oh, I'll just be back for the contest, then I'll be moving on."

Each of the beefy fingers on the brute's hand tightened, crunching the dirty fabric of my jacket along with a good helping of my skin. "Leave town. *Now*. This place has enough problems without you skulking around and making people nervous." He looked me up and down with distaste.

Hot anger sparked in my chest and traveled up my throat to my cheeks. This ogre was starting to get on my nerves. "Only man I see being hostile is you. Don't think you're the first one to try and look tough by threatening the outsider." My pulse quickened. I'd gotten into scraps with plucky bullies before, but this man was large enough to strangle me with two fingers if he'd felt like it.

Well, *fuck*.

***

Apparently, all he felt like doing was tossing me through the old doors of the establishment. My old black coat did nothing to break my tumble, nor did my face. Mud oozed into the folds of my clothing, into my right ear, my mouth.

"And take this hunk of shit with you," he shouted. The almost comedic twang of the Lute sounded off to my left. My pulse dwindled to a crawl, but my resentment rose. Muffled though it was, I still heard the laughter of the big dumb ox as he pulled the door shut behind him

I stood and distractedly scraped the filth from my face with a flat hand. It was no different wherever I went. Every interaction ended with me being tossed into the mud. It didn't matter that I was polite and stayed in the shadows, or that I only fought back against those who attacked me first. A person like me wasn't wanted. Was this what my life was doomed to be? Being treated like a curse or some eldritch abomination because I didn't fit the mold of what these shitheels wanted? Pioneering a new genre of music and being the elf I wanted to be was so...lonely. And the grinding loneliness of life and navigating through it ached more than any pangs of hunger.

"*Murder*," the Lute rasped. Only I could hear the voice, apparently.

I sighed and scooped the alcoholic mud from my ear with a fingernail. "I might want to, but no. It's not worth it." Truthfully, it was never worth it to engage with idiots when they tried to get in my face. I'd done it once or twice before learning better. Despite being pitched into the same muck that I had been, the Lute was spotless. Not a speck of mud tarnished the already gruesome scoring along the body of the instrument.

The promised dusk had finally arrived, wrapping the market square in a shawl of shadow. *Good song title, "Shawl of Shadow"*. My stomach grumbled that it was not.

Around the back of the *Piper King's Pit* sat the privy, a small, dilapidated structure close to the tree line. As bad as the muck had been outside the tavern, it was twice as treacherous here. Like a blackened snowdrift whipped up by wind and left in jagged drifts, the sludge heaped in mounds and valleys that were difficult to navigate.

The door to the privy swung open on its remaining hinge with a squeal, and the stench of bile wafted out into the night. I sighed and ventured in. Floorboards that were no longer hazel in color covered the floor, warped and misaligned. As the wall sloped upward it changed colors, one piece of graffiti blending into the next, blooming with knife-carved conversations, bad jokes, hate speech, lovers' initials, and poorly painted hieroglyphs and guild symbols. Forget the raucous air of the tavern, the privy would have given most anyone a headache from the constant written noise bouncing back and forth off the interior.

I approached the water basin, still surprisingly containing a few inches of water. None of it was clean, and judging by the bile and urine that covered the rest of the interior, likely diseased by this point. A single candle provided a light by which to gaze at the image in the scummy water. The murky reflection of my mud-and-blood-crusted, painted, scowling face stared up at me. The face of an elf that everyone I'd ever met had called a freak.

"*Alone*," the Lute said.

I picked more mud from my ear, "I hadn't noticed, thanks," I muttered. Now even my slipping mind was ripping on me.

A dark hum emanated from the instrument leaned against the only relatively clean wall in the privy. "*Angry again.*"

I was—and getting more so with every word. I had a mind to smash the stupid thing just to end the conversation, but then I would have nothing to play with in the contest of song. No instrument, no coin. My gut groaned, and the sound reached my throat.

"*We help.*"

"What did you say?" I squinted at the Lute. Surely, anyone who heard this conversation would think me insane. Was I really engaging with a fucking piece of wood?

"*You help. We help,*" the Lute said.

"Who is we?" I asked.

"*Us.*"

"Fuck youuu." I rolled my eyes. "How are you supposed to help me? And how the hell am I supposed to help you?"

There was a silence, and for a brief moment, a slight panic seized me. As annoying as it was, as unhelpful as it was, I realized that I didn't want the Lute to stop talking to me.

It spoke, finally letting me exhale my sudden fears, "*You help. Find him.*"

"You need help finding someone. And if I find him for you, you help me *how* exactly?"

"*You music. We help.*"

It was official, I was going insane.

Hushed voices broke my apparent negotiations with the instrument. They approached from outside the privy, along with the squelching of boots in the mud.

"Sir, just come back to the tavern and watch the contest. The townspeople need you to show that Moashanda is thriving," a nasally voice urged.

A softspoken but confident voice answered, "But it's not, Alber. I asked the Pit to throw this contest so that people could forget their differences and troubles, but there's too much difference now. Half the people in town can't even recognize their own brother or sister."

The voice belonging to Alber pressed on. "The contest has begun, if you would but attend for just a few songs..."

*The contest had started already?*

I swept my hand downward and grasped the Lute by the neck, bursting from the privy and tearing through the mud and twilight air. The two men who had been pacing near the outhouse flinched in surprise and stared with confused squints. One of the two wore well-fitting trousers with a matching green gambeson. The garment had a crest of a falcon in flight artfully sewn into it, but the dwindling light made it too difficult to see the details. His blue eyes narrowed, crinkling the forehead beneath a head of dark hair pulled back into a tail.

"State your business, stranger," the man's sturdy voice called. Panting from my efforts to stay upright while running through the mud, I lifted an explanatory finger and leveled it at the tavern. This did not ease the man's suspicions. "Stay right there," he ordered.

The other man—Alber, I assumed—approached me. His flowing robes and blond curls rustled in time to his deliberate gait.

No way were these two assholes going to keep me from that show. I needed that prize. Cold muck numbing my toes from the inside of my boots, I sprinted to the scorched and stained entrance of the *Piper King's Pit*. After leaping up the steps two at a time, I crashed through the doors.

I must have looked like death, corpsepaint smeared with blood and grit, ragged clothes washed with mud and earth. It was maybe the most raw I'd ever looked for a performance.

That was all well and brutal, but this presentation would mean nothing if I couldn't produce the requisite sound. To make things even worse, nobody even noticed this pitch-black entrance because their eyes were pinned on the current performance.

A female bard strummed passionately on her lyre from the stage, her raven hair falling in little ringlets across her face just enough to look perfectly messy. The torchlight of the *Piper King's Pit* dazzled off the sequins of her deep blue, knee-length dress, and the smoothness of her voice undulated throughout the mesmerized patrons. Obsessed taverngoers screamed the lyrics back to her from the front row.

I didn't realize that *she* was going to be here.

Natalya Promptua, the most popular performer in all of Enotia, sang confidently from the stack of wooden pallets that made a stage. Tapered elves' ears and strands of hair framing her smiling face, she repeated the chorus once more so that the audience could keep singing along. What was someone who had performed in front of King Kevan doing *here?* As I waded through the packed tavern, hearing conversations about the depth of her lyrics and the new music she had teased and who she was courting, the only thought pumping in my panicked mind was that my prize money had just eluded my grasp. My stomach gurgled. *Fuck.*

Beside the stage and in front of the tavern's back door lounged a number of other dejected performers who had come to the same conclusion as me. The two men with the fiddles, an old woman in a black gown holding a flute, and even a green-eared goblin with a drum. Sweat beaded each of their foreheads, suggesting they had all finished their set for the night. That meant I was on next. *Fuck.*

At the entrance to the tavern, the city noble and Alber threw open the door, rapidly scanning the crowded alehouse for me. FUCK.

Promptua's hand struck downward on the strings of her lyre, concluding her set and sending the already writhing crowd of elves, goblins, and humans alike into a frenzy. They all looked like a field of wheat in a strong wind. Only some, a fraction of the crowd, remained seated and stone-faced, perhaps hoping to hear something different.

I leaned down, pretending to tune my Lute. "All right, fine. A deal is a deal," I whispered into its pegbox. "If you help me in this performance, I'll help you find the person you're looking for."

"*You help?*"

"I help," I nodded vigorously.

"*Then we help,*" the Lute said solemnly. "*We murder.*"

"What?" I squeaked.

Hands clapped down on my shoulder. My head shot up, expecting to see the city nobleman ready to apprehend me, but it was one of the fiddlers. His unkempt beard scratched my face as he wheeled me around and thrust me onto the platform, directly into Natalya Promptua on her way offstage.

Dried muck from my coat smeared along her dress and arm. I stumbled and waited for the crowd to lynch me for attacking their star.

But to my surprise, her arms enveloped me in an embrace that stoppered my face-first spill onto the stage. To anyone watching, she had simply wrapped an old friend into a calming hug. Fortunately, my corpsepaint hid my blush.

"You all right?" she asked into my ear.

I nodded shakily.

"I had to ask because, well, you're smoking."

"Huh?" A quick glance at myself revealed black tufts of smoke beginning to curl off my coat. It swirled upward and into the shadowed ceiling of the *Piper King's Pit* like sand reversing in an hourglass. Holy shit that was metal.

"We *murder*."

"Right, all good," I nodded. Whatever the Lute was doing, I had no choice but to trust it.

Promptua nodded quizzically and propped me into a more sturdy standing position. "What's your name?"

"Ozzymandias. My friends call me Mandy. Or they would if they were here." *Or if I had any.*

The bardess smiled and turned to the crowd. With a flourish, she grasped my wrist and raised my free hand to the ceiling as if I were a prizewinning fighter, "People of the Pit, please welcome Mandy!"

My introduction was met with displeased stares, arms crossed in disapproval, and a few uncomfortable coughs. To her credit, Natalya Promptua paid the lack of reception no mind, patting me on the back with a delicate hand and wishing me luck, as if that would help. I'd just been kneecapped by the most impossible opening act I could have ever hoped to follow. My gut grumbled loud enough for the front row to hear. Black smog continued to twist and rise from my body as I raised my hand over the Lute.

*I hope you know what you're doing,* I thought desperately at the Lute. The patrons who had remained silent during Natalya's performance continued to do so. The village noble and Alber stood, arms crossed at the edge of the stage, probably preparing to arrest me at the conclusion of my set.

Bringing my hand down in a hammering strum, my smoky fingers collided with the strings of the Lute, summoning forth an explosion of deep, raw noise. It crackled in my ears, threatening to burn away the last remnants of my eardrum like a cleansing wildfire. I glanced out into the crowd to see an entire tavern of white-ringed, incredulous eyes. This sound was evil, harsh, metal...

Everything that I had been searching for.

My hands, almost of their own accord, worked faster, turning the buzzing hum of Death Metal into a blistering whirlwind of notes. The riff sped through the crowd and swirled, expanding to saturate the air. Exhilaration, fear, and anger crashed within my being in thunderclaps that boomed through my abdomen until they reached my throat. Not all of these thoughts were mine. Several consciousnesses fused with my own into words that I screamed in a vengeful howl.

**Deprived of vengeance, life extinguished**
**Hatred fills chalice overflowing**
**Beaten bloody for existence**

Mothers covered their children's eyes in horror. The bar-keep dropped a tray of ales to clap his palms over his ears, leaving the alcohol to spatter and crash against the dirt floor. No matter, it made no sound over my furious sonic firestorm. Charcoal smoke poured from my coat, my arms, my eyes. It billowed upward and curled into terrifying, acrid wings. It passed in front of and smothered the torches, strobing and flickering the lights in a violent dance of light and dark.

**Captured and restrained by string**
**Taken from the mortal coil**
**Forced to bend and dance and singThe world is a traitor**

The unfiltered grit of my Lute was joined by other sounds. Somehow, a blasting, breakneck percussion accompanied the low growl of my strumming. Several patrons' eyes rolled backward in their heads.

**Traitor**

Silent shouts erupted from the crowd as a few taverngoers collapsed, shaking and thrashing as if yanked asunder by demonic puppet wire. The village noble began to rush the stage.

**Traitor**

I gazed through the smoke in horror at the screeching, convulsing people. Their skin bubbled and sluiced over their bones as if it were a wriggling amalgam of maggots attempting to jump from a sinking corpse.

*We have to stop this,* I thought wildly, my senses panicked.

"No. We *murder*," the Lute insisted, picking up on my desire to pull away.

**TRAITOR**

Blood trickled down the back of my throat with the next shriek. My eyes bulged and could only watch as the skin burst off the twitching villagers as though they were bubbles popping. But it was all a ruse, a fleshy façade.

What remained beneath the disguises were skeletal beings with sickly blue complexions. Hairless, noseless, and with another pair of emaciated arms folded against their backs, the ghouls continued to screech and wail, small arms and three-fingered hands covering their pointed ears.

It was the most brutal thing I'd ever seen.

The village noble promptly dismissed any concern over my performance and wrenched his way through the crowd, sword drawn. However, he only managed two steps before a blue hand seized his shoulder. The shapeshifter's head still sported the flaccid remains of curly blond hair. Alber.

As I continued my avalanche of a breakdown, I whipped my head around the *Piper King's Pit*. Confused and terrified townsfolk—some still covered in strips of fake human, goblin, or elvish flesh—gawped in horror at the shapeshifters that until recently had been posing as their friends and neighbors. Nobody knew what to do.

"We *murder*," the Lute insisted.

"Open up this fucking *Pit*," I bellowed, raw voice slicked by saliva and blood. "Fight!"

Wrenched from their shock, the patrons of the *Piper King's Pit* sprung from their seats and engaged the writhing ghouls. Swords and knives flashed, glassware shattered, and tables toppled as a frothing brawl commenced, all set to the whiplash tempo of my performance.

**Prison of strings**
**Pitched aside by cruel indifference**
**Made to wallow in undeath**
**Bloodthirst swallows all memory**

The villagers of Moashanda fell upon the impostors with terrible vengeance. The man who had been the victim of sheep theft threw a haymaker into the jaw of a shapeshifter, knocking several needle teeth and globs of inky green blood onto a nearby table. A woman brought her barstool down upon the back of another. It tumbled into the dirt. The barkeep ran another monster through with a sword, the same grimace as always plastered on his face. Everywhere, townsfolk rended apart their tormentors in a fervor, all blazing within my musical furnace.

Green ichor and viscera splattered the dusty ground, trampled and ripped up by shuffling feet in the writhing mosh of fighting. As the Lute and I reached the climax of the song, an unearthly growl grew in my esophagus until it escaped as a bone-wrenching bellow.

**TRAITOR**

I let the last, deathly note from the Lute hang in the air, stewing with the echo of my final growl. Smoke dissipated, and the torches fully lit the alehouse once more. The people of Moashanda panted and dripped with sweat and green and red blood, as well as exhaustion. The shadow of this ominous takeover, the fear of not knowing who to trust among their friends and family, was lifted, albeit temporarily.

A quick stock-take of the *Piper King's Pit* revealed that the place had been nearly leveled by the brawl. Broken tables and stools littered the damp floor in a shipwreck's assortment of wooden parts. Even a chunk of wood was missing from the bar. A random sword was stuck in a support beam overhead, out of reach from anyone on the ground. Patrons smothered a small fire that had blossomed to life near, but still outside, the hearth. The wooden supports of the building drank in the green blood smeared into them during the scrap. Several detached, pale blue limbs wriggled of their own accord on the ground like lizard tails.

Now *that* was a metal show.

Several men and women held the only surviving ghoul, Alber. The blue-skinned shapeshifter strained against its bonds like a fish in a tangled net, but the ropes held. They sat it in a barstool none too gently and stepped back.

All but the village noble. He stood, several hairs sticking free of his tight tail and jaw set like granite. His green-stained sword still rested firmly in his hand as he approached Alber's impostor.

"Where are Alber and the others?" the noble said calmly.

"You should kill him, Loukus," one voice shouted. A dozen others echoed similar desires.

Still, Loukus stared into the glittery, black eyes of the ghoul, "Where are they? I can lock you up if you tell me, or I can hand you over to them if you don't." He gestured at the furious townsfolk around him.

Bleating and chirping, the shapeshifter studied its surroundings, realizing that its options had run thin. "The cave at the foot of the gorge," it warbled in a squeaky, dual-toned voice that still sounded a bit like Alber's.

This was it, my chance to slip out unnoticed while they were focused on the more pressing outsider. No doubt they would be after me once this conversation was over. After all, I'd just encouraged half the town to destroy the place.

"You there!" Loukus's shout froze me before I could take my first step. This was it. I would be placed in a cell with that creature, and it would take my form like some cheap cover bard.

I took a cautious step backward as the village noble approached me, but my jaw fell as the man extended his hand.

"We owe you a debt, stranger," Loukus said. I couldn't discern the look in his cold eyes, but a less skeptical elf may have classified it as *gratitude*.

Weird.

Taking his hand, I shook it firmly so as to project past the paranoia I felt. Someone talking to me as if I were a person was fairly new. I cast my gaze at the small gathering of faces. They ranged from indifferent exhaustion to small smiles. The most genuine-seeming grin belonged to Natalya Promptua.

Loukus waved his hand and the bartender approached with a small sack. The metallic jingle of honest, actual coins tickled my ringing ears. "Please accept this, from the people of Moashanda," Loukus said.

My eyes widened, "I won the contest?"

"No, this is my personal coin."

"Oh." I sheepishly but gracefully took the pouch. It was a heavier bag of coin than I could ever remember holding in recent memory.

Loukus nodded. "If there is anything that this town can do for you, I will see it done."

My stomach whined.

He must have heard. "I'll have Wendel start the ovens. Some meat pies are in order for our guest." I looked down, embarrassed. Grateful, of course, but embarrassed. I looked to Loukus with a silent plea and his face softened. "Take a few minutes to clean yourself up, stranger. We can talk later," he said.

A furtive glance toward the back door of the *Piper King's Pit* unveiled a completely empty path to outside, which I took immediately. The open air greeted my sweating, clammy skin like an old lover, but I couldn't let it soothe me for long.

I once again ran for the privy. Its familiar slant and enclosed walls allowed me to fully purge the emotions that swirled in me like the black smoke I had somehow exuded during the performance. The near-expended candle fluttered near the water basin.

A gleeful yell charged out of my open mouth before I had a chance to formulate any words in my mind. The sound I had searched for—and when I couldn't find it, yearned for—had finally become a reality. No longer would I have to endure the dainty, small sound of a traditional lute. This instrument and whatever lived inside it were the answer to everything.

But the brutal lyrics from that song had not been mine.

I hefted the Lute in front of me. Its bright red appeared even more luminous in the dark privy. "The person you want me to find, they trapped you in there, didn't they?"

"*Yes. Shadow magic. Find him.*" Shadow magic? Anyone who used that arcane atrocity would be hung. It involved stealing souls and forcing them into servitude. What had I gotten myself into?

"You helped me, you gave me the sound I've wanted my whole life," I said, the words catching in my bloody throat along with a lump of gratitude. "I swear I'll help you find him. We'll confront him together." For so long, my loneliness had chipped away at my soul, and for once, I had met someone—or something—that was in a more miserable state than myself. The instrument and those trapped inside had fallen into my hands, and I felt responsibility weighing on my shoulders for the first time in years. I was all the Lute had.

The Lute hummed in agreement with my pledge. I set it down gingerly and clawed some more dried mud from my clumped hair. "What is his name?"

The Lute paused, "*Don't know.*"

Well, that was fucking brutal.

# The Scarecrow

# &

# The Lover

# The Scarecrow & The Lover

I never expected to be furious at an audience for sticking around.

However, my payment for this gig depended on them cutting and running. Scratchy, golden cornstalks swayed all around me. Tassels atop the plants tickled my chin and dumped pollen and aphids across my frayed coat, making it difficult to perform without sneezing or itching.

My audience fluttered from stalk to stalk, chittering in a taunting rattle and occasionally glancing up at me with beady, black eyes. Some openly cawed and hooted with laughter. Instead of displaying a cautious or fearful demeanor, the crows flitted through the black smoke of my performance as if frolicking in some cheerful rainstorm. Many others bobbed their heads as they hopped along the floor of the cornfield, picking up stray kernels with their shiny beaks. I screamed, lyrics falling on indifferent ears.

**My tormentors, callous to all**
**Pick the carrion from the earth**
**Swarm in demonic thrall**
**To the hunger and thirst**

"*They won't leave,*" scoffed Lute. For the first time, the instrument sounded exasperated. I slammed my hand downward against the strings, strumming violently. Cornstalks flattened before me. Dry snapping rapidly applauded my blunder as hundreds of plants collapsed to the earth with a rustling sigh. The crows rocketed into the sky only to dive back to the dirt and pluck all the new kernels I had jarred loose. This was brutal. The riff was good, but the lyrics needed work.

> **Pick my veins from my wrists**
> **Like twigs from the dying fields**
> **I banish you from this land**
> **This realm that will never heal**

Jeering caws heckled me from every conceivable direction. Impatience seethed from within Lute and billowed out into the crisp autumn air, creating a malevolent mirage that blurred my vision. Blobs of midnight-feathered shitheads lurched between the stalks.

Moving on from Moashanda had been a mistake. The problem, however, was that everyone there was still petrified of me. Oh, I had saved the town from those skin-shifting ghouls, but everyone still remembered how I had done it. The fair townsfolk walked around me as if I were a heaving anvil weighing down the ice on which they all walked. No one wants to be exploded, and the prevailing fear was that I could do that to anyone. I wasn't one of them.

But for one night, it had felt like it. And that had been over a month ago.

More stalks collapsed around me as my self-pity bubbled into anger. They were all afraid of me. Everyone except these godsdamned birds.

**Laugh to the sound**

**Of my misery**

**fucking erase**

**Every vestige of memory**

Pitch black smoke roiled through the cornfield, blanketing the crows jittering along the ground. It did nothing to cover their caws. I still heard them, somehow, over Lute's grainy hailstorm of a tone.

"*Hate crows*," the instrument growled.

I wordlessly agreed, moving my calloused fingers along the neck, letting the strings breathe and blur. My fingers ached, small burns forming from where the pads of my skin slid along the bare metal wires—my haphazard replacement after the last strings had broken. Two days, this performance had lasted.

Ragged coughs and gags floated toward me through the smoke. It must have looked like the field itself was burning, but it was just me. Smoke remaining from a fire that had never found purchase at this venue. The coughing grew closer.

**Murder...the murder**

**Murder...**

**The murder**

"Excuse—" another fit of coughing interrupted the speaker, currently just a vague humanoid outline in the smog.

I expelled the last of my energy into a lethal growl, grinding the back of my throat into a warm paste. Smoke evaporated and wind greeted my face again after somehow being diverted throughout the performance. I was starting to get a feel for whatever power Lute held. Their consciousness lapped against mine like calm ripples around a fishing boat. Not just one but multiple minds resided inside the wooden body. All were put there forcibly by someone that I had no hope of finding, or any clue where to start.

So once my coin had run dry, it was back to finding odd jobs, and when a Death Metal Bard couldn't book a tavern, the job of scarecrow was a humiliating second place.

"*Must find him,*" Lute insisted.

I groaned. "I know, but you haven't given me anything to look for! If we're going to travel the land aimlessly looking for this cretin, we need coin."

"Who are you talking to?" a voice piped from the trampled corn.

I looked up from Lute to see a young man hacking and waving away the remnants of the soot. His tawny and tangled hair fell down to his chin, and the excited stubble of a young man who had recently gained the ability to grow it prickled from his jaw. A short sword hung at his hip. All in all, he and I looked the same age, but there were decades between us. Elves age slower, after all.

Instead of answering his question—too much to explain—I squinted down at him from the stump I perched upon. "You're the farmer's son, aren't you?"

He nodded, strong chin jutting out, "That's right! I was inside the house when my father hired you." He shifted uncomfortably, eyes scanning the desolation I'd wrought to the crop. Mangled stalks like crunched bones, mud and dirt squelching in an earthy gore, black crows traipsing through the wreckage. It was as metal as it was likely that I wouldn't be getting paid.

"Look, kid. About this..." I gestured around me.

He snapped out of his horror at my work, "No, no, no! I'm not here to criticize you. I actually came here for your help. And I can pay you too!" His eyes glimmered with something like hope.

"Pay?" Lute snapped to attention. Coin would bring us opportunity, which would allow us to travel further.

Which could lead us to Lute's betrayer.

Hopping down from the stump and straightening my bad posture, I set Lute down against the pedestal and strolled to the lad. Someone in Moashanda had patched up my boots, so the mud stayed outside them. The bottle of *South of Heaven* whiskey that the tavernkeeper of the *Piper King's Pit* had given me bounced against my hip as I walked, attached to my belt by a thin sash of rope.

The farmer's son leaned away from me slightly as I approached. Perhaps it was the corpsepaint, or the earthy smell that always accompanied my clothing, or the pollen-slapped wardrobe that made me look like a grouchy tortoiseshell cat.

"I'm not going to eat you, kid," I snapped. Maybe a bit harsh, but I was tired of people treating me like some defective firework with an unknown fuse length.

"Sorry, I just didn't expect you to look...like this," he said. "My father said that you had runes carved into your forehead, and that you had a forked tongue, and had eyes blacker than midnight in the Shadowlands."

*Black eyes, that's a new one,* I thought. I shook my head, keeping my very emerald eyes open and trained on the lad.

A crow picked that exact moment to land on my shoulder. I glared at the bird and rolled my shoulder, shaking it off. I didn't care how metal it was, those birds were on my shit list. "You said you wanted my help or something?" I said, trying to steer the conversation back to the point.

His face brightened, "Oh, right! I require your services as a bard."

"I'm listening."

"*We're listening. From over here,*" Lute huffed from their stump.

"I plan to propose to the love of my life, Korinne, tomorrow morning. And, you see, she loves music more than anything. And I found out that you're a musician..." He trailed off.

An alarm began to chime in my head.

He took a deep breath. "I would like you to perform while I propose to her." He puffed out his chest, as if it had taken all his strength as a strapping young farmhand to tell me this.

"*We'll go,*" Lute said solemnly. Thankfully, only I could hear them.

I scratched my head with sore, exhausted fingers, "Listen...what's your name?"

"Patroclus. Call me Patch." He extended a hand.

"Mandy." I shook it. "Look, Patch, I don't do the romantic stuff that people play for their lover. I play Death Metal."

"Death what?" Patch asked.

"The music I play. I like it, and it works for me, but it's too dark and brutal. You heard me just now."

"Love can be brutal," he said.

Pinching my fingers over the bridge of my nose, I shook my head. "Look, I'm not saying...I just don't think it's a good idea." This kid wasn't understanding the core concept of a love song. Death Metal just wasn't the right genre. Honestly, the fact that he wasn't getting this foreshadowed a doomed proposal regardless.

"Please, you're the only bard I can find around, and she leaves tomorrow morning," he pleaded. "After that she'll be gone for three months. I can't wait that long. Once you know you want to marry someone, you just can't hold it in." His clear blue eyes glinted in desperation. "I'm prepared to pay you all I have." He undid the flap to a burlap bag slung across his shoulder and dug out a crinkled, cinched pouch. Metal coins slid over one another softly as he gave it a gentle shake. It was so big it required two hands to hold it.

Lute grumbled expectantly, *Take it.* They knew we had nothing left to travel anywhere unless we planned on walking another sixty-some miles to the next town. No food, no water, no coin.

I held out my hand, expecting him to shake it, but instead Patch plopped the coin purse into my hand with a casual gesture that was almost a toss. The sides of the bag drooped over the edges of my palm in a weighty, metallic frown. There was no way Patch was just *giving* me this amount of currency in advance.

"That half now, the other half when you get me to Korinne's cabin," he nodded. "No point in waiting around, either. We'll head out right away."

I allowed the corners of my mouth to twitch upward and inclined my head forward in agreement. Lute waited impatiently by their stump. Caws and rattles sounded off in a needling staccato from every crevice of the field, either begging me for an encore or sneering me off the stage. I didn't much care which.

We set off into the waning gold of the sunset, Patch, Lute, and I. As we exited the field and placed our feet upon the parched dirt of the road, I waited for the kid to direct me: either south toward Bloria or north toward Hurlan. Those were the only two real directions. This woman's cabin was likely to be on the road to a settlement. A puzzled jolt shocked me from my thoughts as I watched Patch cross the road and crest the hill on the other side.

I called after him, "Hey, kid! Where is your lady's cabin again?" He'd never given me a location, only that it was less than a day away. Scrambling up the hill and nearly losing my footing in the pulpy grass, I arrived at the apex of the hill only to be greeted by an icy pang of worry.

The lad was leading me and Lute into the Birchward.

It loomed a hundred feet in the air, the pale trunks of birch trees packed together tighter than an overcrowded bone-yard. Color drained from the air just at the edge of the tree line, making the inside of the forest a smattering of whites and various grays. These trees grew thick and tall, much more so than that of regular birches. The canopy above strangled any potential sunlight and left the forest floor in an eternal night.

Metal, but what the fuck?

I caught Patch just before he could step across the tree line. "What are you doing?" I yanked his shoulder back, jerking his body around to face me. Lute hummed in my other hand. "You didn't tell me that Korinne lived in the Birchward, kid."

He rolled his eyes and scoffed, "Nobody lives *inside* the forest, Mandy. She lives on the other side of it. This happens to be where the forest is thinnest. We can cut through it and get to her cabin on the other side before breakfast tomorrow." He pulled an unlit torch from his satchel.

"There's an 'if' that you're forgetting there," I scowled. This forest was an unspoken forbidden frontier. Anyone who ventured in eventually donated their bones to the white tree limbs that grew ever upward. Some said that the more creatures that perished in there, the taller the trees would grow. Despite my nerves, I reminded myself to write a song about that.

"Look, she leaves tomorrow evening, and it would take days to go around. You don't have to come with me, but then I'd like my investment back," he said, hand jutting out. He let the threat hang in the air, but it was a thin one. His fingers trembled in anticipation for me to devour him or dismember him or something. I just shook my head. This lovesick fool was going to get me killed.

But it was better than sitting on a stump with those crows.

"*We're going. We'll make coin. Then find him,*" Lute insisted. The instrument's vocabulary had grown of late, and the maximum capacity of these sentences they could utter into my frazzled mind had gone from two words to three, all in about a month. I couldn't forget the reason we were taking this commission: Find the man who had trapped the spirits I conversed with inside that wooden prison. Lute's crimson gloss gleamed in the diminishing sunlight but became muted once we crossed the threshold of the forest. I silently hoped that the grim woods would let us pass intact.

"*Murder,*" Lute cautioned.

"What?" I whispered from the corner of my mouth.

"*This place. We feel murder.*"

Immediately as we set foot inside the trees, gooseflesh crawled up my arms, and the overwhelming sensation that I was not welcome in these woods radiated from every ghostly trunk. The feeling of watching eyes stabbed into my back, but I trudged on. Better to be paranoid and moving than paranoid and still.

For a while, the dread proved unfounded. I plucked absentmindedly at Lute's wiry strings and contemplated what romantic lyrics lurked in my head. So far, nothing.

"So tell me about this Korinne," I said, hoping for a distraction from my creative block. "What's she like?"

Patch grinned as we trudged over the gray, near-grassless forest floor. "She's funny. Sarcastic most of the time, but it's got this sincerity to it, you know? Always got this twinkle in her eye that tells you you're in on the joke, even if you don't get it. You don't see much of that in rangers."

"She's a ranger?"

He nodded, puffing a bit as we climbed a gradual slope. "That's why her cabin is so close to the forest. It's not really hers. It's an outpost that she's meant to occupy and guard the countryside from beasts. Lots of things lurking in the forest that could wander out and cause trouble."

A sarcastic ranger was pretty raw, I couldn't deny. Part of me wished she was in here with us, keeping an eye out. But then I remembered that her presence would require me to play the love ballad that so far had eluded me.

*★★★*

Only an hour had passed before we glimpsed our first monster. A troll, shadowed and far off in the distance. Thin, stringy hair draped over a squat skull, and its mammoth frame seemed to move in slow motion in that way all gigantic creatures do. Patch and I ducked behind two nearby birches and waited, breathlessly, for the troll to tire of whatever it was doing and leave. It didn't take long. Trolls have the attention span of a toddler. As the thumps of its footfalls receded into the distance, Patch and I exchanged a glance. With luck, we just might avoid the horrors of the Birchward. If we made it out in one piece, *that* would make a brutal enough song.

Unfortunately, our luck couldn't last.

Somewhere that Patch swore was over midway through the forest, the ground softened, and moisture began clinging to the outside of my boots. Pale gray moss clung to the sides of trees, to boulders, and increasingly to my feet. Standing water burbled more and more with each step we took. We had walked straight into a bog. I stood and overlooked the swamp while Patch gripped his torch tightly. I could have done without the bright beacon that signaled our every move, but humans apparently can't see in the dark as well as Elves, so I decided to let it go.

The bubbling water and silt stretched as far as my eyes could see, and sprawled just as far in front of us. Birches twisted at impossible angles from the marsh like broken bones healed askew. Blotches of mud beckoned us forward, crooning some illusion of safety while probably concealing sinkholes and damp crevasses. The stench of gas reached my nostrils.

"*Metal*," Lute observed. I nodded in agreement, drawing a confused look from Patch.

"Well, on we go," Patch said nervously. He took a single step forward onto a stripe of silt that looked solid enough.

The moment he set foot on the surface of the muck, the bog before us detonated into a typhoon of brown water and gritty sludge. Between droplets of black rain that spattered my eyes, I registered two massive silhouettes rising from the swamp, birthed from mud and shadow. Guttural grunts and deep-throated warbling passed between the two leviathans as if communicating. Slimy, pockmarked skin gleamed in the flickering torchlight. Coal-black pupils regarded me and my traveling companion with dispassionate hunger. Claws extended from webbed paws as the creatures stood on their hind legs and sloshed through the bog toward us. Heavy croaks, deeper than even the lowest-tuned instrument, rattled my heart within my ribcage. I didn't hear the croaks, I only felt the vibration.

Patch throttled the hilt of his short sword and ripped it from its scabbard. The rusted blade still reflected the torch's radiance in small blotches.

"Kid, what's the plan here?" I shouted through the muck that now covered my face. Lute had miraculously remained untouched from even a speck of filth.

Waving his torch and sword savagely at one beast as it lumbered in his direction, the lad looked wildly for an answer. "Play something! Try and scare them off!" he yelped. The creature towered over him, easily twice his size.

Right. I hefted Lute and felt the collective consciousness of the instrument bleed into my own. A fiery yet cold fear had gripped me: a fear of this place, of dying in this bog, and of the pot-bellied, amphibious monsters that stood before us.

And rage at the audacity of fate to put me in this situation.

"*Murder.*" I wasn't sure if it was Lute or myself who had spoken.

The feeling coursed through my body in a whirlwind. It filled my lungs and burst forth in an unearthly scream. Another tidal wave of mud and water exploded outward, but in the other direction. The toadlike goliaths were pummeled by a wall of silt and moss, which hurled them backwards into the swamp and threw them down. A gargantuan smack thunderclapped through the trees, along with the evil sound of my strumming. The rhythm of this riff took off in a jagged, syncopated frenzy as midnight smoke poured from my form.

It had only been a month, but I'd begun to understand how the power within Lute worked. The spirits that swelled within the blood-red wood responded to how the strings were played. Play faster? The aura it created would thrash in a frenzy. Play slower? It would create a foreboding doom, creeping ever forward. It lasted as long as my arms, fingers, and voice could stand.

I had been playing all yesterday and today, but my fury and desire not to be eaten doused my limbs in liquid fire, and the smoke roiling off them responded in kind

Each rivulet of smog rising from my frame twisted and convulsed in a spidery tentacle. Wicked, angry, dangerous.

These behemoth toads were about to have a bad day.

Patch's eyes grew in horror, threatening to pop from his skull and fly into the bog. Only the competing gain of the creatures' furious croaks broke him from his terrified trance. Hefting his sword, the kid prepared a charge, head bobbing with the riff. Whatever happened, I had to keep Patch alive. He was the backline of this performance, and I couldn't handle two of those things at once. I doubted that these fiends had the same weakness as the shapeshifters from Moashanda.

Only a few moments and the behemoth toads were upon us again, but this time we were prepared.

**Feel your blood join the bog**

**Streaming back to the earth**

**To the mud where you were born**

A coiled, barbed tongue shot just past my ear and crunched into a birch trunk to my left. Venom dripped from the appendage and coated my shoulder. Even though the fluid didn't puncture my skin or infiltrate my blood, the skin under my coat tingled and burned. I ignored the sensation and concentrated on making my fingers a blur along the neck of my instrument. The lick of rapid notes spurred the smoky hurricane around me to swat the tongue away. Heavy percussion beats vibrated along marshy ground.

Not ten feet away, Patch dodged a swipe from the claws of the other swamp-dweller. He spun on his heel and hacked at the wrist of the monster. His blade bit into the bone and nearly lopped the whole hand off, spewing a fountain of black blood.

Metal.

**Rotting flesh, a feast**

**Vengeance for the flies**
**Maggots eating tadpoles**
**Before your helpless eyes**

The toothy gums of a behemoth toad loomed over me, and a deep, growling croak roared a challenge. I responded with a howl of my own, and the smoky tendrils coiling around me sharpened, becoming feral. Slimy mucus coursed over the abomination's skin, the stench wafting into my nostrils and nearly making me gag through the lyrics.

"Mandy! Help!" A cry of pain from Patch distracted me. The other amphibian held him aloft by his ankle, claws digging into his flesh. In the frantic light of the torch, I saw growing rivulets of blood working their way up his leg. His captor grunted in victory, tongue slithering from its maw, ready to wrap him up and swallow him whole. The stench of gas hit my nostrils.

I eyed the torch, still in Patch's hand and burning much too low. A webbed, three-toed foot squelched in the moss just in front of me. I stepped backward, avoiding a grab from a slimy paw, "Patch! Throw the torch!" I growled. The riff sped up in desperation.

The kid somehow heard me. With blood from his own leg dripping onto his face, he hurled the firebrand into the bubbling bog behind his captor. For a moment, I thought that the light had gone out completely.

But suddenly, the ghostly blue flicker of flame raced across the ground. It ate up the moss voraciously, leapt across the mud, reached its tendrils towards the gurgling bog...

Azure became bright orange as an ear-rending boom shook the forest. Timid flames that were content to stay on the marsh floor mere moments ago now greedily reached for the canopy.

**Feel the fires of perdition**
**Tearing at your soul**
**Pulled downward by the bog**
**Melting your frail bones**

I blinked aggressively to rid my vision of the afterimage burned into my retinas, but the sudden shock of the brightness filled every crevice of my eyes.

The only thing I could see through the radiance was the shadow of the predator standing before me. The behemoth toads shrieked at the sudden inferno, green skin now a sickly, pale color as the heat drained them of the moisture they craved. To my left, Patch—released by his captor—rolled through the mud into a kneeling position. As the toad that dropped him clapped its webbed paws over its eyes, Patch lunged upward and drove his sword through the top of its open mouth and into its brain. Inky blood sluiced over his hand, and he released his grip on the sword. The off-kilter death croak of the beast became a gurgle as it fell backward into the muck, dead.

The sharpened coils of smoke around me weaved and dove as I slammed my fingers against the strings. I felt a little too much give in one of them and the string snapped with a ghoulish twang. I felt Lute shriek in the back of my skull, but we both kept playing.

**Let your blood feed the bog**

The behemoth toad turned and fled just in time for the smoky, black tentacles to impale it through the back. A strangled squeak escaped the monster's deflating vocal sac, but

I hammered Lute's strings again and again. The monster's blood spattered across my face while the shadowy claws twisted it apart. Limbs and sinews split like wet papyrus. Slimy flesh drooped to the ground, and the toad's ribs and vertebrae snapped inward one by one as the fumes from my Death Metal pulled it inside out.

I blinked through the ichor and released my hands from the strings just in time to see an unrecognizable amalgamation of gore and bones smack into the now-ashen bog. Blood rushed in an exodus from the corpse, watering the remains of the burned moss and pooling around my boots. My legs buckled from underneath me and I sat down hard in the gory mud. A metallic sweetness spread across the back of my throat, and I hocked the blood from my mouth. Whether it was the creature's or my own from growling, I didn't much know or care.

"*Brutal*," Lute groaned. I actually felt the instrument *shudder* in my hands. A single, bloody tear trailed down the wood where the string had snapped.

"I'm sorry, Lute," I whispered. I had pushed them too hard. Immortal spirits trapped in a wooden body or no, I needed to respect the instrument more.

Lute refused to answer.

Was it even worth it to get the coin at this point? Would it really benefit us to play metal and likely sabotage a proposal if we even made it out of here alive? We had the first half of the payment, and that would be more than enough to get us to the next town. It wasn't worth making more people afraid of me. I could already see Patch's white eyes underneath a face full of mud, warily looking me up and down. I had shown him what Lute and I were capable of, and it terrified him as much as it had the villagers in Moashanda. Fermented scents reached my nostrils and I realized that the bottle of whiskey around my waist had shattered, spilling alcohol on my pants and snaking slivers of glass into my thigh. *Great.* At least the sack of coin was intact.

Patch groaned off to my left, prone and dripping with blood that *mostly* wasn't his. The lad retched, yellow-brown bile spurting out from behind his teeth. What a fucking disaster of an adventure this had turned into. I stumbled on weak and exhausted legs toward him, boots slipping in the muck. My fingers dribbled blood from where Lute's frayed strings had burned and cut them, the brutal consequences of metal without rest.

"We aren't going to make it, are we?" he panted.

I shook my head, wearily peering around the Birchward. It was only a matter of time before some other horror became curious and decided to investigate the bright fires and deafening noise. "I can't believe I let a bag of coin and a lovesick idiot talk me into this," I muttered.

"Look, I'm sorry, Mandy. I was wrong to ask this of you. You just don't know what it's like," he said, voice trembling. "You don't know what it's like to have to be apart from your person, to feel that little thorn gouging into your heart a bit more every day."

"That sounds more like a heart condition." I rolled my eyes. What was a little needle compared to emptiness? At least his life had someone in it.

Patch's muddy face flared in anger, "Oh, make fun if you want. I don't give a damn what cynical bullshit you do or don't believe in. All I know is what I feel in here," he tapped his chest, "and it's like a fresh hole is torn there every day when I realize a whole world stands between me and her, even if it's technically less than a day's journey." He gestured around him at the forest. "The hole gets bigger every day, and it's *bleeding*. I have to do this, *today*, before it all runs dry and it leaves me a husk."

My dumbfounded eyes widened at the kid, watching his angry, labored breathing. His leg and face twitched in spasms of agony, but his eyes never left mine and never lost their determination. Lute, finally breaking their silence, hummed quietly beside me.

"*That's metal.*"

They were right, it was the most raw, brutal, fucking pitch-black thing I'd ever heard. I needed to write a song about this.

I *could* write a song about this.

The gears in my mind creaked into action. The creative block crumbled, and a tide of possibility flooded my mind, carrying riffs and growls and solos and breakdowns. It was possible. If we could just get out of the forest alive...

I could make true love *metal*.

From beneath my boots came the slightest tremor, rhythmic and unsettling. The ashen moss quivered and stood on end as if it were the hairs of some hyperaware prey. The vibrations quickened and amplified, bringing the swamp to a panicked, frothing dance. What I recognized to be giant footfalls were headed right for us. Couldn't we have just five minutes between each fight for our lives?

Using one arm, I scooped my hand and wrist under Patch's armpit and hauled him upward, drawing yelps and curses from the lad as he stood on his bad ankle.

"Can you run?" I hissed.

"What?"

"We need to go. *Now.*"

Not a moment after I shot those words from between my teeth, the birch trees behind us shuddered and were peeled aside in a sickening, forceful crunch. Massive fingers, dirt clotted between folds and callouses in the skin, grasped the trunks as if they were broom handles and casually shoved them aside. The uprooted and fractured skeletal trees groaned and buckled. The crash as they landed shook the bog, and Patch, Lute, and I stood face to face with a troll.

Its sunken, yellow eyes glowed dimly in the light, regarding us with dim-witted surprise. Perhaps it had mistaken our racket for something of a bigger size that could challenge its territory. Fortunately for it—and decidedly not so for us—it had found two wounded morsels maybe worth using as toothpicks.

A gust of wind ripped upward into the air in one mighty sniff of the troll's mangled nose. Most of it was missing, leaving a ghoulish cavern above its mouth. The neck and ears were swollen in hematomic bulges that were undoubtedly the result of years of wrestling and challenging other trolls. Its bulbous mouth dripped with famished saliva. *I should have stuck to battling crows.*

"I can definitely run," Patch said.

A treacherous and preposterous obstacle before, Patch and I blew through the bog with relative ease as the troll began its pursuit of us. The marsh was much less of a concern. Bone-white trees blurred in my periphery. I thought a silent apology at Lute and brandished the instrument, jumbling fingers trying to position themselves over the strings.

"*Do it. Play!*" Lute shouted.

I strummed the fastest riff of my life, notes shooting in rapid bolts through the dense silence of the forest. Echoes reached back like an unruly audience. Patch's gait intensified, spurred on by the tempo. Black smoke whipped off me and faded away as I sprinted. Some adrenaline reached my limbs, like it had from the battle with the behemoth toads, but the energy was sapping quickly. The haste was wearing off. *Performing nonstop for two and a half days will do that.*

I stole a glance behind us to see the troll gaining. Its stringy hair dragged along the ground in matted coils, a consequence of its bent back tilting even farther to try and snatch us up. My brain conjured images of being squashed to paste between its fingers, ground up by its flat, yellow teeth.

Barely any smoke was flowing from me now. The noise of Lute's grainy distortion remained, but the usual performance was lacking. I was missing notes, and my fingers couldn't keep up with my legs. Gargantuan footfalls pounded the forest floor mere feet behind me.

"There!" Patch screamed. "The edge of the forest!" A slight aura of warmth registered at the edge of my beclouded vision. I saw it: the place where the trees ended and the world outside—safety—began. Stepping out into the light of day could save us, for trolls hated direct sunlight.

We had just reached the tree line when the beast caught us. I felt the dreaded, immense pressure of its grubby hands a second before one closed around me, and I looked on in dismay as the kid struggled in the grasp of the other. Even if I had the energy, there was no way for me to use Lute to get out of this. My right arm was pinned inside the troll's fist. My left held Lute upward in a defiant salute.

"*Find him*," Lute pleaded.

"I..." I choked, almost as much on the stench as from the hand tightening.

"*Must find him*," they urged again. I realized that they were begging me not to die, but I couldn't keep my promise. Black spots appeared and rapidly devoured my vision. The troll was going to squeeze us into bloody powder.

I didn't feel myself hit the ground, nor did I hear the angry bellow of the troll as it let me go, but my returning vision caught the orange brilliance of flames. As I wheezed and rolled onto my back, I witnessed the goliath trumpeting in agony and rage while trying to pluck a flaming arrow from its eyeball. The milky white of its eye rapidly became a dark brown, a rotten egg frying in a skillet.

A determined voice knifed through the creature's diminishing howls, "Now what the *fuck* is this mess?" My jacket bunched under a vice grip, and I felt myself dragged the mere twenty yards to be free of the Birchward. The deafening bellows of the troll faded further into the forest and away from us. Knotted, bony trees glared down at me, the survivor who shouldn't have been. But survival hadn't been my doing, it was the mysterious person with the sharp tone. An elbow brushed my bruised ribs and I swore, turning my head and seeing Patch in the grip of the rescuer's other hand. Somehow, we'd registered as a man and an elf in the eyes of our hero, and not the swamp-filth banshees we likely resembled.

For the life of me, I couldn't see the reason why the kid's spirits had lifted. No doubt he felt the same as me, likely worse. That leg needed serious attention, and he was probably nursing several cracked or bruised ribs too. Once light hair had been dyed black by the Birchward and its horrors. But all the same, the dried mud on his face cracked and flaked off as he smiled wider than a man crowned king. "We came to see you before you left on your mission!" he said brightly.

"I'd gathered that, thanks. Great to know that I was the reason for this suicide attempt," Korinne growled. "I don't even go into the Birchward overnight, and never that deep. Do you have any idea how easily you could have died? What would I do then?" A slight tremor shook her scolding voice. She dumped us on the downward slope of a grassy hill. The sun hung directly over us. It appeared our estimate of arriving by morning was optimistic. Relief bloomed through my chest as I tightened my hand and found it still gripping the neck of my instrument. Lute hummed in my fist.

Our rescuer looked only a year or two older than Patch, but her tightly braided hair was stark white like the trees we had just escaped. Stern, gray eyes flicked between the two of us with a mixture of worry, disbelief, and a healthy amount of anger. A quiver of arrows hung around her shoulder, and a longsword was strapped tightly to her hip.

Patch eyed me nervously, obviously wondering if he had fucked up too spectacularly to continue with his plan. I shrugged and immediately regretted it as pain shot through my ribcage. We were here. Too late for him to go back on his plan now. The lad's eyes set in determination, and he shakily stood, wobbling and keeping most of his weight on his good ankle. "Korinne, this is my friend, Mandy."

Friend? My eyes widened beneath the blood, muck, corpsepaint, and exhaustion.

"And I brought him with me because I needed to see you before you departed, to ask you something." Patch's face melted into a smile, a confident, loving grin that seemed to quell some of Korinne's well-placed anger. He looked to me, still sprawled on the hillside. "Do your thing, Mandy," he nodded.

Right. I scrambled to my feet, hurriedly brushing myself off and then realizing it wasn't worth it. Gore, mud, sweat, slime, and all manner of substances cemented and hardened to my clothing and hair in the sunlight. Lute vibrated in my shaking and exhausted hands as I held the one-string-short instrument at the ready. Clouds of gray vapor leeched off my body as I strummed a driving, deliberate intro. My sapped strength didn't afford me nearly the spectacle or gain, but it would have to do. The ghastly sound rolled through the sodded field and incline like an approaching thunderstorm. I nodded back to the kid, and he took Korinne by the hands.

"Korinne, we traveled through the forest to get here because the Birchward doesn't scare me. Not as much as it would to spend my days without you," Patch said, voice rising to be heard over Lute and I.

Meanwhile, I growled the greatest love ballad ever written.

**Heart is palpitating, bursting**
**Lips are heavy, sweating, thirsty**
**Beauty instills fear of time**

**Sweetly decaying to slime**

The ranger said nothing, eyes growing wider with every word that Patch spoke. Wind tossed the lovers' hair as the moment, my song, and the whole world swirled around just them. A piece of toad-flesh slipped from a fold in Patch's shirt and plopped unceremoniously to the ground.

"You're strong, and sarcastic, and hilarious, and everything I could ever hope for in a companion. I feel safe with you, and the world is a better place because of you."

**Love possesses souls forever**

**Cannot exorcise my fervor**

"Korinne Jarlmundt, will you be my wife? I swear to love you until my dying day, and to *never* set foot inside the Birchward again," Patch smiled tearfully.

**Be with me**

**Until you die**

The last vestiges of my performance ricocheted off the countryside, echoing "*die, die, die*" for miles around. And then, complete silence. Korinne's face went to an unreadable place, as if she was trying to cling to the anger she still felt at him for so stupidly risking his life. I waited for the ranger to tell him off; to curse in his face and storm away.

But as tears welled in the young woman's eyes, all she could muster was, "You hired a bard?" Without another word, Korinne pulled Patch to her and kissed him. I breathed a sigh of relief and let my legs collapse beneath me, finally allowing today's—technically the day before *yesterday's*—performance to end. Patch melted into his woman's arms and their happy tears dissolved into bubbling laughter.

"*They're strange*," Lute mused.

I grinned, "Yes, they are."

Korinne pulled away from Patch and brushed some of the grainy silt from his face. "You realize that you'll be making up for this little stunt for years, right?"

"Oh, of course," Patch chuckled. His ankle twitched, but it couldn't dent his beaming smile.

The lovers continued their quieted conversation, and I let myself fully sprawl backward onto the hillside. Every muscle I was aware of—and even some I hadn't even known I had—ached terribly. Blood clotted around the wrinkles of my knuckles, and my throat finally gave up on producing anything that resembled a voice. I was spent, and I felt Lute's consciousness vibrate with the same exhaustion. The first of our new coin would have to be spent on new strings for the instrument and some more whiskey. Glancing again at the couple, I shook my head and ignored the pop that came from my neck. By every right, Patch should have been devastatingly binned for a multitude of reasons. Showing up just as she was about to leave, hiring the worst bard for the job, nearly getting himself killed by charging headlong into a forest that she had constantly warned him against.

But the ranger loved him anyway. His stupidity, his poor planning, and his foolhardy bravery did not change that. Something stirred in my chest as I realized that if she could see past all of these faults and love the lad unconditionally, then perhaps someone out there could feel that way about me. A stupid dream, but a pleasant one. I smiled hopefully through the new pattern of corpsepaint that the pollen, bog, and blood had created. I shook my head, slipped my fingers into the coin pouch that Patch had given me and fished out a gold and silver coin each.

Lute's muted consciousness suddenly blazed to life in my ears. "*That's him*," they snarled. I wildly scrambled to a sitting position and whipped my head all around. My eyes scanned the countryside. This was brutal timing. How were we supposed to fight this asshole in such a dismal condition? My ribs flared in protest.

"Where?" I said a bit too loudly. Korinne and Patch separated and reached for their weapons in alarm, warily searching for the cause of my outburst.

"*In your hand*," the souls within the instrument steamed.

The two coins glittered in my palm, reflecting the golden sunlight. King Kevan's face raised a regal eyebrow from the gold. A curly head of hair and closely trimmed beard framed his squared, determined jaw. For a moment, panic spiked through me as I thought that Lute was insinuating that the king had done this, but something in the angry, jumbled thoughts cascading against the hull of my brain made me dismiss the notion.

The man on the other didn't assuage my fears.

Smirking from the polished silver coin was a thin-faced man with shoulder-length hair that the mint had done a fine job of texturing. Shivers crawled down my limbs when looking into those eyes. Despite having seen many coins exactly like it—although not as many as I would have liked—never had I paid enough attention to the actual man on the coin to see those unnerving eyes. Even stamped into metal, they sneered with unknown motives and taboo knowledge.

It was the face of the king's mage, a man named Emile Gurren. My dry mouth suddenly became a desert. "Lute, are you sure this is him?" I asked, not even attempting to hide that I was talking to a piece of wood anymore. Patch and Korinne tilted their heads in confusion. Maybe they were more alike than I had given them credit for.

"*That's him*," Lute said, "*Emile*." An eerie tremble snaked through my body as the spirits spoke his name with the same inflection as a deathly curse. The king's mage practiced shadow magic? "*Find him. He must pay*."

A tuft of smoke curled from my hand as I closed my palm around the coins, now much heavier to hold than they had been without this knowledge. It wouldn't be easy; I would likely be bringing the wrath of the kingdom down on my head if I wasn't careful. Not to mention that Lute and I were now hunting a fucking *wizard*.

But I'd promised, and this little music box of spirits was the closest thing I'd ever had to a friend before Patch. Having awoken the souls within, the responsibility of their revenge had fallen to me.

"It doesn't matter who he is," I growled. I let the coins slide from my hand and back into the pouch, cinching it tight. "What he did to you is wrong, and he's going to pay."

Lute hummed in agreement, "*He will pay. And it will be metal*."

I set my jaw and nodded, "You bet it will."

# PERFORMANCE III

# DECLARE WAR FOR A LYRE

# Declare War for a Lyre

My coin and whiskey were sufficiently low enough to be dangerous.

The extravagance of the king's city of Cloverhold was almost as legendary as its high prices of living. The inns and taverns cost twice what they had in the country, and every one had been keen to kick me out after a night or two, resulting in a tavern-hopping routine that I'd grown quite sick of over the past week. After having made friends in country folk like Patch and Korinne, I noticed that city dwellers so far had shirked any archetype of being friendly toward outsiders. It wasn't as if the last five months since the Birchward had been unfruitful or even uneventful. I'd played several shows in villages and towns that dotted the long road to the Cloverhold, earned my share of profit, and gained what a generous person might have labeled "applause."

But my stomach still insisted every night that it wasn't enough, slapping down any sense of accomplishment. Together, my gut and Lute made quite a team.

"*You need to find Emile,*" they insisted.

I set my whiskey down against the hard wood with a louder thunk than I had intended, drawing a few wary eyes to my booth. Even though I looked better than I had in months, the assessment was by *my* standards. Fresh paint adorned my face in a newer, bolder pattern that sharpened my eyes and cheeks. Every button was perfectly fastened to my new hemp coat. The garment still stained my hands from the extra black dye I had poured on it. It was already a dark, deathly hue, but I'd wanted it even blacker.

"We're here in the city, aren't we?" I asked in a low voice. Increased interaction with others hadn't quelled the feeling that Lute was one of the few beings who would voluntarily hold a conversation with me. It compelled me to keep speaking with them at the risk of sounding mad. "This city is where Emile is bound to be, but the king's mage isn't going to just entertain anyone, *especially* not someone accusing him of trapping souls in a block of wood with shadow magic. Best if we lay low and rest, keep an ear to the ground. We can make a plan once we know more."

The whiskey slipped down my raw throat and soothed the inflamed vocal cords. By far the best stuff I'd had since getting to the city, this batch. What had the barkeep called it? *Slick Leg* or something. Strong notes of brown sugar and caramel danced across my tongue, but not potent enough to be overpowering.

Lute's impatience continued to grow from the seat across from me. *"You've drank one cup already. What's the point of a second one? Waiting for some drunken wisdom? We're wasting time."*

"Try some," I dipped my fingers in the glass and flicked droplets of alcohol at Lute. Childish, but I was getting sick of their restlessness, and their newfound ability to chastise me in full sentences didn't help. It'd been seven months since I'd acquired the instrument, and I distinctly felt all nine souls that were held inside the confines of their timber prison. I felt them every minute of every day, their confusion, and their *anger*. So much raw emotion churned inside Lute that I was convinced they needed Death Metal as much as me.

The *Troll's Head Tavern* made for the most brutal atmosphere of any alehouse I had seen in the city thus far, mostly due to the decor. The skull of a troll, nearly as big as the one Patch and I had run from, hung behind the bar. Room keys hung on rings from its bleached-white teeth. Below the skull sat a library's worth of dingy, ornate, and cracked bottles intermingling in an orgy of shelved toxins, booze enough to drown an ox. Talons, fangs, and bones of various sizes jutted from the walls or dangled from the ceiling, all brought here by rangers after killing a monster. Crudely carved initials decorated the warped paneling beside each trophy, making history of the kill. Pretty metal if I said so myself. I'd given up after a mere five minutes of trying to find anything resembling Korinne's name. Oil lamps adorned each table and booth, some leaking fuel onto the bench. I'd steered clear of those ones. Flyers of scratchy papyrus were nailed to the door, most displaying the likeness of a missing woman named Quelenna.

A scrawny jongleur piped on a flute off in the corner, playing some song apparently written by the king himself. Kevan's songs were always popular, always requested, and never subtle. I couldn't really complain, though. Nothing about what I played was subtle.

"Who *do we know that might have information about Emile?*" Lute said, calmer this time.

I shook my head and cast my gaze in a wide but discreet arc around the inn's sparse patronage. Our prospects were zero or perhaps even less. Most had gone to bed by this hour. The once blazing brick oven of the tavern was now blackened and hollow. It was near impossible to think that anything had once cooked, or even existed, in that sorrowful maw. I fished a crumpled bit of parchment from my coat, ignored the ink stains, and found a clean corner to jot down *sorrowful maw.*

A squat, bony hip jarred mine out of the way and shook me from my concentration. A small drop of whiskey dribbled from my cup and onto the pockmarked surface of the table. I glared angrily to my right and saw no one.

"Ahem," a gruff voice coughed.

I adjusted my gaze downward and saw a stern-eyed goblin scowling back at me. A stout knife hovered inches from my belt line.

I blinked slowly, letting my new corpsepaint do most of the grimacing for me, "Can I help you?" I was met with grim silence. Tufts of graying hair protruded from the goblin's temples, his chin, and his nostrils. But his sharp and suspicious brown eyes didn't show a day of age. Who was this asshole to just sit down in my booth and threaten me?

"Oh, come on, Ord. He's a friend," a familiar voice said from across the booth. The person spoke in a hushed tone, as if hoping to not draw attention.

Ord did not lower his knife.

I sipped my whiskey, "You heard my friend, Ord." After making sure I had emptied the glass, I squinted over the table at my "friend."

Smiling back at me was Natalya Promptua. I risked smudging the face paint I wore to rub my eyes and look again to make sure it was actually her. The most famous bard in the land sat across from me, elbow to strings with Lute. A deep purple robe draped over her with a cowl hanging low over her face, but I'd seen that grin up close, and I wouldn't forget it anytime soon. She fidgeted with her ringed fingers absent-mindedly. "Sorry about him, Mandy. He's a good bodyguard, but he doesn't take much opportunity to relax."

Flattered that she remembered my name, I flicked my eyes sidelong at the goblin. "Seems like he picked the wrong person to guard if he wanted to relax." I didn't have to explain what I meant. Natalya's social circle was a carefully picked one, and numerous—and quite public—instances of her dealing with unwanted and obsessed hangers-on gave me no reason to question why.

She sighed and nodded, her thin hood flapping a bit. Faint shadows from the lantern washed over her chin. "It can be difficult sometimes, but I like to think it's worth it at the end of the day."

"So what brings you to my booth?" I said, catching myself staring at her bright red lips as she grimaced. I angled forward in anticipation as she swiveled her head from one end of the *Troll's Head Tavern* to the other. She leaned in and I caught a whiff of lily scent.

"I've been looking for you," she said. "Ever since I found out 'The Death Bard' was in town, I've been searching all the taverns." Her eyes glimmered from under the cowl, wreathed by ringlets of raven hair. "I'm in need of your services. I realize that this isn't normal, or ideal, or...practical," she paused, leaning back and brushing Lute's newly strung neck, "but I need your help."

My brow furrowed in confusion, likely making the white-and-black pattern painted on it crinkle like an accordion. "I couldn't have been your first choice."

*"Can she help us find Emile?"* Lute vibrated. Natalya noticed the movement and eyed the instrument warily. I nodded for her to continue.

Natalya rubbed her brow and sighed. "I was specifically looking for you because you're mostly unknown in this city. What we're doing could bring a lot of scrutiny, and anyone with even the smallest amount of recognition here will be targeted. For better or for worse, I'm the only one who knows you here. If you need to go to ground, you can."

I wasn't sure if I should have been flattered at her concern for my well-being or annoyed at being called unknown. Either way, my now always-ringing ears refused to tune her out. The kindness she had shown me in Moashanda was more than enough goodwill for me to hear her out.

"My lyre has been stolen," she said. "By my former manager."

"You have a manager?" I asked.

"*Had* a manager," she corrected. "Zephyr Vossen. The man's a monster, and he doesn't handle it well when people tell him no. Turns out that he *really* doesn't like it when he gets fired. A month or so ago, I told him I was letting him go, and he threatened to make me miserable."

I considered this, certain that I had heard that name before. "Where do you think he's keeping the lyre?" I asked.

She paused and glanced at the other patrons, still fiddling with the rings on her fingers. The Natalya that I sat across from was not the one I had been propped up by in Moashanda. She was nervous; some might have said scared. "He's likely got it in the Vossen Estate," she said.

Now that rang a particularly ominous bell. I apparently hadn't hidden my shock well enough, for she nodded grimly.

"Prick's got a fortress," Ord said gruffly.

I leaned back in my seat and made my best attempt at looking unimpressed. Behind my cool demeanor, my mind worked furiously. Lute and I had been through some shit, but there was no guarantee when trying to storm a castle, no matter how fearsome. "I assume we have others helping us in this rescue mission?" I said.

"Just us three," Natalya said. "Zephyr has too many important friends. Half of the king's court is in his pocket. It's a small operation by necessity, not by choice." Fucking perfect.

"*Who on the king's court is in his pocket?*" Lute hummed. His question shocked me out of the conversation with Natalya, and it seemed to have some effect on her as well. Her eyes flicked toward the possessed instrument. It was possible that another elf could sense the gloomy arcane aura they exuded, or maybe even could hear them speak. I repeated the question to keep her suspicions off Lute.

She shrugged, "Who knows? Not really a big fan of any of them, if I'm honest." Her head tilted in such an alluring way when she shrugged that it almost jolted me from my train of thought. It was a long shot, but it was possible that

Zephyr Vossen knew how to find Emile. It would be stupid, dangerous, and short-lived to storm a stronghold with just two elves and a goblin, but I couldn't deny that my heart rate began a dangerously metal beat in my chest at the thought. Lute and I *were* planning to kill a wizard, after all. Taking down Zephyr could bring us a step closer to the elusive Emile, not to mention lend a hand to a talented, virtuous, wonderful musician.

Had I called her wonderful? Odd thing for me to think. Ord must have read my thoughts. The stout knife pricked my elbow, just enough to sting like a motherfucker. I jerked my arm away and glared at him, getting a scowl in return.

"*He doesn't like you. Should we murder him?*" Lute asked.

"No," I said quickly.

"I completely understand if you don't want to take part," Natalya said disappointedly. "It'll be dangerous, and—"

I shook my head vigorously, "That's not what I meant! I want to help. I truly do. It'll be brutal. We'd be happy to help a fellow bard."

Natalya and Ord squinted in confusion.

"Brutal?" Natalya asked.

"We?" Ord said.

This conversation was going to be the death of me if it went on much longer. "I'm in. Just tell me when and where," I said.

A hand closed around mine and rested on the table, and I looked up into Natalya's sincere gray eyes. Her hood was pushed back just enough for me to see her whole face when up close. Gratitude bloomed upon her statuesque features. My cheeks felt so warm that I feared my corpsepaint would melt off.

"Thank you, Mandy. You're a true friend," she said. "Meet Ord and I near the gates of the city at sundown. We'll walk to the Vossen Estate grounds from there and sneak in while it's dark. Do what you need to do, warm up that voice of yours, and then let's take this prick down and get my lyre back." She and Ord slid from my booth without another word, flipping the barkeep a silver on their way out. The barkeep blinked several times, trying to discern whether the woman he'd seen had actually been the woman he'd seen. Lute and I slouched in our seats, letting silence take over the room as the jongleur in the corner finished his set and counted the few coins tossed to him throughout the performance—one of which had been my last silver.

"*Friend?*" Lute said.

"Shut up. Let's just get another drink and then go. Sundown is in another hour or so."

"*And then we murder?*"

I hailed the barkeep and waited for another glass of *Slick Leg*, "If it calls for that, yes."

***

Less than an hour later, I walked on sober-enough legs toward the gates of Cloverhold. Twilight had set in, and the shadows lengthened like weeds. While most would have been frightened of being snared in them, I kicked through them without a care. Since Moashanda, I'd felt increasingly at home in the embrace of the umbral. The crisp spring air stung like a sharp knife. *Maybe Ord's knife. That shit really hurt.*

Lute hummed in my hand, and I used a finger or two to distractedly pluck at their new strings. Certainly the finest strings I'd ever purchased for an instrument, the sturdy and thick wires were coiled and wound with animal gut. Lute had groaned nonstop when I affixed the new accessory to them, but there were no complaints now.

An assortment of humans, goblins, and elves removed themselves from my path—and my periphery—as I strolled toward the gates. Though it usually upset me to think that most people were afraid of me, it would be one of my biggest strengths tonight. Easier to take on a fortress if the people guarding it are scared stiff of you. Luckily, I'd written some material just for the purpose of creating a terrifying atmosphere. We passed by a post displaying more papyrus flyers of Quelenna, the missing woman I'd seen displayed in the tavern. The name slipped in and out of my mind, feeling familiar all the way through. Someone didn't get that kind of reach unless they were important.

Cloverhold captured a beauty that few other cities could. Sandstone-paved streets, oil lamps at each corner, ornately stained wood trim on each house and business; it was a city permeated by extravagance. A nutritious bedrock soaked through with lively lifewater. It was undeniably gorgeous. But it was too polished, too straight-edged, too *mainstream*. While I had enjoyed my time drifting from tavern to inn here, I couldn't see myself living in the kingdom's prized garden of society.

Even the most fruitful gardens had weeds, and we would be battling with one tonight. Stealing an instrument from a musician was an especially heinous misstep that set my teeth grinding. You were stealing their livelihood; a source of their income and comfort. Perhaps most importantly, you were thieving a part of that person's soul. I knew deep in my gut that I would plan an especially brutal consequence for anyone that dared to try and steal Lute, and Lute would no doubt exact revenge of their own.

As the gates drew nearer, I registered two cloaked figures leaning casually against the walls of the city. The cobblestone barriers enveloped them in a shadowy veil, and it took a blink or two of elven eyes to pick them out amid the darkness. This rescue mission would be dangerous for me, but Natalya would be in another world of shit if something went wrong. Best to not attract attention, lest the darling of the kingdom ended up a victim of gossip parchments. The things were nailed to every post, every work board, every tavern and temple door. She could become a pariah without even getting the chance to explain herself.

"Good, you made it," Natalya said. Even in the low lighting, I could see her relieved smile.

Ord grunted, as if acknowledging that I had arrived but stating that he wasn't exactly happy about it.

"*Murder?*" Lute said.

I closed my eyes to avoid rolling them and slid into the shadows with Natalya and Ord. "So, what's the plan?"

Natalya anxiously twisted one of the rings on her left hand. "The Vossen Estate is just a short walk from here. From my time with Zephyr as my manager, I visited a few times and got a sense of how things are laid out there. I even discovered a secret entrance or two if I needed to get out unseen," she said.

"So," I said, "if we go through one of those secret entrances, it's less likely to be heavily guarded since it's secret?" She nodded and set her jaw. I glanced at Ord, waiting for him to say something, but the goblin may as well have been a stone. Albeit a very threatening stone. His wool cloak did a fine job of hiding the plethora of knives stashed along his person.

With an unspoken signal, the group of us stalked off into the night. To most performers, it would have likely seemed odd to stick to the shadows and blend in rather than draw eyes, but I'd been blending into hostile environments for most of my life. Sticking to the darkest corner of any place was how I managed to avoid getting thrown out or worse.

Natalya's feet crunched in the grass as she neared me. "I never asked you how you gave your instrument that tone." She nodded at Lute. "Is it some kind of enchantment or spell?"

"Oh, I..." I stammered. What the fuck was I supposed to say?

"Is that why it talks?" she asked.

A bolt of panic seized my muscles for a moment and I froze. She could hear Lute the *whole time*?

"*Do we have to murder her?*" Lute growled.

She laughed and waved away my mortified expression. "Don't worry, your secret is safe with me." Her laugh was music in of itself, a bright sound with a hearty tone that suggested laughing was one of her favorite pastimes. "Sometimes I wish I could speak with my lyre. You're a lucky person, Mandy."

I nodded uncomfortably. "Lute hasn't been so lucky. I promised to help them find someone." I proceeded to tell her everything. How I found Lute, how they started speaking to me, and my promise that I would assist them in their vengeance against Emile. Natalya was silent throughout all of it, and I realized that I'd never considered breathing a word about Lute and my partnership until now. Speaking with another musician, especially Natalya, felt freeing.

"That's horrible," she said, glancing at Lute. "I'm so sorry that happened to you."

*"We'll make it right. There's a special Death Metal song just for him. Right, Mandy?"*

I nodded, a flush of emotion swirling in my chest.

We snuck down a side street until a tall, iron gate loomed over us by several feet. The gate and wall surrounded an expansive plot of land and a manor that wished it were a castle. Its fortified parapets and stony gray walls whispered of renovation, and gaudy banners flapped atop each of the three towers as if signaling "the King is home". Not very subtle. Fucking unsightly, actually. I already disliked this poser.

"All right," I said through gritted teeth, "where is this secret entrance?" My expectations were high, and Natalya didn't disappoint. Followed by Ord, she nonchalantly edged down the cobbled street toward a string of granite statues. Each one had been carved with a careful hand, depicting people with wide brows, self-important smirks, and a warhammer in their grasp. The way Natalya scowled at one of the effigies suggested that this was the Vossen family.

Lute hummed loudly as the prospect of another performance became more tangible.

After glancing around to ensure we weren't being followed, Ord and Natalya approached the grandest and newest statue.

It was obviously Zephyr; I didn't have to ask. The statue's physique appeared grotesquely enhanced by the sculptor, with a tunic that was conveniently torn down the middle to expose a muscular, granite abdomen. Curly hair fell to his shoulders.

Natalya gripped the stout base of the likeness and heaved it to the side while Ord prodded from the other end. Despite its apparent immovability, the statue slid along the cobblestones with a hollow grating that sounded not unlike my most rudimentary metal growl. Not that this wannabe warlord could likely produce a musical note if his life depended on it.

Underneath the false statue yawned a cavernous maw in the avenue, and a ladder leading down the murky throat. Faint torchlight flickered at the bottom with the frailty of a butterfly's wings against the inside of a jar. Whatever light was down there was scarce, but two elves and a goblin would have no problem adjusting to the lack of light. The short, rickety iron ladder led us to a damp stone floor in a tunnel that stretched farther than I could see in the dim light. The single, red torch covered the damp ground in a crimson blood-like sheen. To either side, the walls glistened with slime. The mouth above us had led to a gruesome gullet.

A hand gently rested on my shoulder, comforting. "The tunnel has a few bends. It used to be a sewer system before Zephyr had it bricked over and turned into a secret passage," Natalya said. She smiled reassuringly. "I never liked it down here. Glad to have you with me."

I nodded, unsure how to respond and feeling a blush under my painted cheeks. It was in that brief look from her that my resolve to carry through with this mission steeled. At times, my bitterness or frustration toward popular and beloved bards had made me callous to the idea that one would ever befriend me, but Natalya had upended this notion from the very start. The lens through which I filtered the world to make sense of it had always been either raw or not raw. Metal is soulful, unfiltered, and unquestionably bold—everything that this woman embodied. Natalya shared nothing in common with me, but was in a way more brutal than I could ever hope to be.

"*Someone's coming,*" Lute warned. I steeled my nerves and gestured with my chin down the gritty tunnel. Natalya and Ord braced themselves behind me, Ord brandishing a knife and Natalya gripping a club, ready to thrash.

At the edge of the torch's bloody luminescence, the figure of a guard swam into focus. A sword hung loosely at his belt, and his head craned forward as if trying to discern if we were merely a trick of the light or actual intruders. "Who goes there?" he shouted.

An evil grin split my face as I held lute, my fingers itching over the strings. Time to put into practice what I had written. Plucking at the gut and wire coils, I coaxed pitch black smoke from the instrument, letting it twist past my knuckles in a nest of snakes. The serpents billowed further and slithered down the length of the corridor until it swallowed the bloody torch, the sentry, and the very sense of up and down. All the while, Lute snarled a grainy, foreboding tone that crawled along the walls in spidery dread. While slower than our typical death metal, this song was meant to terrify. It was a slow march, doom personified. Creeping death.

**Hear the death rattle's call**

**The grim scales ringing hollow**
**A wail shambling closer**
**Hissing its quarry's name**

All light in the tunnel was snuffed out, letting only my growls and Lute's ghastly din prove that existence hadn't been completely devoured.

But for the guard, the abyss would have been better. The methodical riff and undulating smoke enveloped the man, muffling his shrieks and tearing where his limbs thrashed. Like an undead python, the tendrils of smog coiled over his body, locking it in place and sending him to the ground in a wriggling lump, a mouse caught in its deadly embrace.

**The crawling end**
**Sinks its teeth in your soul**
**Extracting the blood from bone**

I stalked down the corridor, willing the screeching lacerations of Lute's harmonics to expand and penetrate the molding of the walls, the very bricks that held the squat ceiling aloft. Natalya and Ord followed me cautiously, her hand on my shoulder and his hand gripping the tails of my coat. They likely were as blind as the poor sap who had been stupid enough to work for an entitled nobleman. However, I saw a clear path through Lute's fumes to a rounded corner. More voices pinged off the slimy brick walls as we approached. The necro haze of distorted sound muffled them.

"*Murder,*" Lute said.

**The serpent slips**
**Around your neck**
**Feeling panicked breaths fade**
**Strangled by darkness**

Footsteps battled with the performance of ruin and lost, all smothered by the sound and Death-Doom Metal exhaust. Smoky serpents encircled four more guards as we strolled through the tunnel toward the Vossen Estate. The men squirmed and thrashed against the fumes until the coils slumped them to the ground for an involuntary nap. Natalya's nervous breath blew strands of hair off my shoulder. Midnight smoke curled along the ceiling of the burrow in such volume that it appeared to drip from the stones like black blood.

The meandering, haunting riff took on a dour and explosive breakdown, sending the tendrils shooting toward the end of the tunnel. Through Lute's collective consciousness, I confirmed that no more guards stood in this corridor. I allowed the song to dissipate and dropped my hand from Lute's strings. Bloodred torchlight overtook the blackness in a tidal wave of clarity, and along the corridor lay unconscious guards, some with swords still in their scabbards. Rageful scorch marks adorned the walls, etching the name *Emile* hundreds of times. Lute's anger was getting stronger, more articulate.

"Gods above," Ord cursed, dark eyes widening at the aftermath. This little display was likely to make him distrust me even more, but we couldn't afford to linger. Already, a few of the guards had begun twitching as if waking from a nightmare.

Natalya forged ahead to the end of the tunnel, coming to what was much more of an iron slab rather than a door. She dropped the club she carried to the damp floor and fished a pin from her cloak. Before I realized what she was doing, Natalya stabbed the rusted lock on the door, jiggling the mechanism in an attempt to undo it. Her lips pursed in concentration, and I found myself observing her battle with the door with interest until a muted click undid the lock.

"You've certainly got the trick of this place," I said. *Why did I say that?*

She shrugged, "I've been here just a few times, but enough to remember how to get in without making a stir. With any luck, those will be the last encounters we have before we steal my lyre back. However, you might have to play another "Doom-and-Gloom" song on the way out. Will you be able to?"

"You've got it," I nodded. As long as Lute was in my hand and I had the physical ability to play, there would be no problems. I dropped one foot into the room and felt my boot depress a brick in the much drier floor. As the block descended further below the floor line, a rumble shook my bones and raised gooseflesh in a ripple across my limbs.

*"That's a fucking problem,"* Lute said.

One by one, the bricks in the floor crumbled from underneath me, individual teeth disintegrating from hungry jaws that yawned open. Before I could leap back, I was gobbled by the beckoning blackness. My companions' hands clawed for my coat and my arm, but my momentum was sufficiently great to actually drag Ord over the edge with me.

*"Mandy!"* Lute's voice shot through my brain before the instrument and Natalya's desperate fingers slipped from my grasp, leaving the instrument in her hands. The cry drilled into my mind so forcefully that when the voice disappeared, my head felt hollow, empty, and alone. Clay and dislodged

mortar battered me and Ord as we tumbled into the aether of whatever lay below the secret tunnels of the Vossen Estate. Blood trickled from my mouth, and a sharp pang iced over my arm at the sensation of a rock colliding with my elbow—or perhaps it was Ord's skull. I had no time to make sense of the true bludgeoning object, for the darkness swallowed my senses and I knew nothing more.

***

I woke amid the rubble and dust, hacking and groaning. In the dim light of whatever shithole we'd fallen into, my eyes barely registered Ord's bleeding face. I looked back up to where we had fallen from and immediately wished I hadn't. Some indeterminate distance above us, a rugged square of light cut through the blackness. It was as if someone had snipped a piece of pale parchment and pasted it to the dark ceiling. Too far up to climb, and nothing to climb up with. Brutal.

Ord groaned beside me, "I think my rib's busted, you halfwit! What kind of fool thing were you planning to do, just walking in like that? Vossen may be a thug and a thief, but he's not an idiot."

"How was I supposed to know that he had the tunnel rigged to collapse?" I said. The pain in my elbow had morphed from a sharp pang to a needling numbness. I massaged the spot where either a rock or Ord's head had clubbed me; hard to decide which of the two would be harder. My eyes slowly made sense of my surroundings, and like a fog clearing with the morning sun, the dust finally dissipated.

We stood amidst a graveyard of likenesses; statues abandoned in various states of decay. Many held instruments and some held swords, while others clutched scrolls with the same propensity of wielding a weapon. I shuddered at the frigid realization that this was where the effigies of Zephyr's former clients went to live. *And what about the clients themselves?* A crude wooden door was set into the rocky wall of the cavern. I waited for a jibe from Lute, for the instrument to say something that would cut the tension and ease my harried nerves, but nothing came. Lute had been dislodged from my grasp, and I could hear nothing. No one.

I was alone again.

The feeling punctured through my bones and nerves, tingled my skin, and made my heart plummet into my bowels. The metal was gone; the blackness, rawness, and brutality had drained from everything. There was nothing, just hollow loneliness after seven months of having nine spirits in my head.

"We have to get back up there," Ord said with more urgency than ever could have been expected from the grouchy bodyguard.

I sat there, listening for Lute. And heard nothing.

My cheek didn't register the first slap, or the second. It was only when Ord wound up for the third, corpsepaint and ink from my jacket staining his hand, that I finally moved and pushed him away. Words didn't even escape my parched, painted lips, just an anguished grunt.

"The fuck is wrong with you, lad?" Ord hissed. "Natalya is going to soldier on with or without us, and no one can go up against Vossen alone. She asked you for help, the Kaans only know why, and you don't get to sit and blank out on her."

"My Lute…" I muttered.

"Is likely with her," the goblin finished. "That cursed instrument of yours means a lot to you, I know. But what do you think is going to happen if Natalya is caught? You can either help her get back her lyre *and* your instrument, or you can lose them both to Vossen. And we would likely die too."

Molten rage seeped into my blood like water through hemp. That would *not* happen. Lute and I still had a job to do, and I would be damned if Vossen got in the way of that. "Right," I said. I spat a gob of blood from my mouth along with a couple molars and raised myself to my feet. The urn's worth of dust piled into the folds of my coat billowed into angry clouds as I straightened the garment. I stood as a silhouette amongst the gloom, dormant and seething.

"So, what are we going to do?" Ord asked

The dust came to rest on the ground, revealing my snarl, coated in rage and smeared paint. "We murder," I said.

Creaking and wheezing echoed across the cavernous graveyard of sculptures as the warped door swung out on oil-starved hinges. Before Ord and I ducked behind a pair of carvings, I glimpsed the shapes of at least four men rushing into the space. Perhaps they were Vossen's men sent here to finish us off. I heard the ring of metal sliding out of sheaths, the cautious patter of boots tiptoeing through rubble, the gusts of anxious breath.

But loudest of all, I heard my blood pulsing within my ears in a furious blastbeat.

The first of Zephyr's thugs fell, Ord's knife sprouting from his shoulder. A panicked scream climbed the sloped walls of the cavern, but just like these thugs, it would not escape this tomb.

As the next one rounded a pile of marble limbs, I leapt from behind my cover and swung a sculpted leg into his shin. The bone snapped like a dry twig and sent him tumbling into the dust. At the height of his scream, I plugged his wailing mouth with the gritty marble toes and leaned over him.

"Where is Promptua's lyre?" I demanded, my performance growl trickling into the question.

The man's eyes bugged, and he squirmed with terror upon seeing my warped corpsepaint and mangled hair. It was probably the most raw and horrifying I'd ever looked. It was just a shame that it was here and not onstage. I peered without blinking into his dusty face, waiting for an answer. A string of brown spittle trailed from the marble foot when I took it out of his mouth.

"Upstairs," he gagged, "in the display vault with all the other artifacts."

"Other artifacts?" I narrowed my eyes.

He nodded frantically. "The other instruments or items he takes from those he works with. It's probably there."

So the poser had done this before. How many other musicians, artisans, and creators had he stolen from? Judging by the decaying statues around us, this had been going on for years, perhaps decades.

I pointed the chipped leg at the thug's chest. "Are you going to stay here, or do I have to introduce you to my friend over there?" I gestured to Ord, who was busying himself with methodically wiping the blood from his knives. The other three guards no longer made noise. It turned out that Ord was scary as shit.

The man nodded.

"Where are we going, kid?" Ord called.

I rested the leg over my shoulder. It was brutally heavy. "Display vault. Upstairs." Leaving the last thug to cradle his splintered leg, I kicked through the rubble toward the open door. Already, a special song for Zephyr had begun formulating in my head.

Without another word, Ord and I stomped through the marble rubble and across the threshold of the door. A rickety, splintery staircase stretched upward, breaking our view as it bent around a corner after around a hundred feet. Ord took to the lopsided stairs immediately, and I trailed a few steps behind. Nails stood upright out of the wood in sparse obstacles, and every step brought a frightful creak from the structure as if tormenting the staircase.

But the vibrations from our careful footsteps weren't the only things shaking the stairwell. A deep, primordial succession of chords permeated the walls, circulating around the space as if it were a convection of heat.

"Natalya," I gasped. Before I could deduce any more, Ord and I were taking the crude stairs in multiple bounds. Before too long, I had overtaken him with longer strides. My legs pumped in the same tempo as the defensive riff that Natalya was undoubtedly playing on Lute's strings. It was a good rhythm, and I could tell that she was making the most of the unfamiliar sound. The building blocks were there for a solid metal performance.

As we reached the top of the shaky stairwell, a trio of guards appeared above us with drawn swords. Their confident snarls disappeared as Ord brandished his long knives and I wielded my leg. In half a measure, my marble limb crunched against their knees and sent them tumbling down the wooden stairs. Ord's knife flashed, catching them in the back of the neck on the way down in a ribbon of crimson. The gore spattered unevenly on the stone walls. One step collapsed as a man's shoulder slammed into it, causing him to nearly fall through the stairwell into some unknown abyss.

We flew up the remaining steps and burst into an ornate hallway with opal floors and ceilings high enough to anger the gods. Perhaps I should have been more impressed with the scale and majesty of this pompous abode, but it was too crisp. All spectacle and no character. A *Piper King's Pit* or a *Troll's Head Tavern* felt much more homely than this. This was a pristine mausoleum, a tomb for a lineage too stubborn to recognize its own death rattles. I placed the foot of my battle-leg on the polished flooring and leaned on it like a cane, panting. The brutal exertion of falling into a statue cemetery and then making a raw-as-fuck comeback was definitely taking its toll.

Too short to reach my back, Ord patted my thigh. "We're close now, kid. Let's go get those instruments back." Nodding, I heaved myself off the leg and sprinted after the goblin bodyguard toward the scratchy warnings and metallic screams of my Lute.

No more guards blocked our winding path to the display vault. Gaudy paintings of Vossen ancestors adorned the hallways, intermingled with even worse paintings of Zephyr posing with powerful people. Natalya, King Kevan, Emile...

I skidded to a halt on the squeaky opal flooring, eyes widening under the paint, blood, and grime. So the poser *did* know Emile. My blood flowed like lava under my skin. "There you are, bastard," I growled. Even when painted in oil, Emile gave a knowing smile, taunting me.

*That's right*, the painting smirked. *Close, but not close enough.*

"Mandy! Come on!" Ord shouted from up ahead. I shook myself out of the vengeful revelation and burst into the vault alongside the goblin.

A forest of pedestals greeted my dumbfounded gaze, each one topped with items that ranged from junk to treasure. A fair few even held barbarically restrictive terrariums, holding live creatures captive in a cruel display. Some I recognized. Most I didn't. My sight slid quickly from the trove of artifacts and landed on the source of the defensive metal that echoed through the domed hall.

Far at the other side of the space that looked like it had once been a ballroom, a crowd of some thirty armed mercenaries surrounded the most famous bard in the land. Torchlight reflected in Natalya's harried and furious face, glaring off the drawn blades and axes that hovered, anticipating a slaughter. For now, they appeared preoccupied with Natalya and Lute.

I glanced to my right to see Ord slinking to the nearest pedestal, raising a clawed hand toward the hourglass that rested on the platform. Its blue-gold frame supported a glass body that looked to be holding...snow? That didn't seem right.

"*Mandy, get the lyre,*" Lute's voice weakly shot through my head. My legs almost buckled right there. Hearing the voice of my friend brought a wave of relief flooding into my limbs. Luckily, I was already resting on the battle-leg. Natalya's head perked up slightly, just enough for me to notice that she'd heard Lute speak to me, but not enough to tip off the people that surrounded her.

"*The lyre,*" Lute insisted.

"Thank you for bringing in another artifact for my collection, Natalya," a self-important voice echoed through the vault, traveling up the walls that had clearly been painted and carved to host parties rather than hoard treasures.

I crept to a plinth two artifacts away from where Ord and I had entered. A silver lyre with reflective strings that gave off a light blue sheen had been haphazardly placed atop the column. It was the same stunning instrument I had seen her play all those months ago in Moashanda, and here it was, stashed away to never see the light of day again and never make another sound. Warmth spread along my fingers as I gripped the instrument, and I silently hoped that I knew what I was doing.

"Give me back my lyre, Zephyr," Natalya said coldly. Her gray eyes glowered at the man pacing impatiently behind the threshold of thugs. The only thing that his statue outside had gotten correctly was his wide brow, but the retreating hairline, average height, and tight silk tunic over a frame that suggested more parties than battle spoke of a privileged ostrich.

Zephyr chuckled as if Natalya had said something much more amusing, "You are in no position to bargain, my dear. If you'd retained my services, then perhaps we wouldn't be here, would we? I suppose I can't persuade you to hire me back, can I?"

Ord and I crept closer to the standoff, him holding a knife and the snowy hourglass, me with Natalya's lyre and my battle-leg. Natalya spat at the feet of the thug nearest her.

Zephyr sighed, "Then I guess we don't have a choice."

"No." Natalya shook her head, red lips in a hard grimace. "We don't."

Quick and light as a sparrow, Ord whipped the hourglass from his hand in a sidewards motion. The contraption flipped end over end once, twice, and shattered on the back of a sellsword before it could complete a third rotation. Shattered glass and metal framing was swallowed as the snow within the hourglass expanded exponentially, crackling and hardening. Centipedes of ice crawled across the back of the unfortunate man, wrapping him in a frostbitten embrace and spreading to either side of him. Before anyone could blink, three thugs were encased in a twisting bondage of frost. Their wide eyes and open mouths shrieked silence within the glaze.

As Zephyr and his guards whirled around, Natalya slammed her fingers down upon Lute's strings, unleashing a vengeful tidal wave of black, smoky bile from Lute's body. The force of the dark chord hurled several of the mercenaries backward, pinwheeling and crashing into the plinths. The guards frozen by the hourglass shattered on impact into bloody icicles. Ruby red shards glided over the polished floor in all directions. Objects perched atop the columns crashed to the ground. One simply fractured and broke, another burst into flame, and another emitted a diabolical laugh and began leaking green steam.

"*Open up the pit,*" Lute beckoned.

I set my fingers into a dissonant chord along the lyre's strings and ripped my hand outward, creating an ear-melting crash of tones with Lute's earthy roar. It turned out that more than one song would be needed today. "Here we go again, motherfucker!" I screamed. With the tail end of my howl, I bunched my legs and leapt upward, ramming over a much larger podium that towered in front of me. The terrarium resting at the apex of the stand wobbled, plummeted, exploded on the ground, and released what I had failed to notice resided within it.

A slumbering juvenile dragon, encased in a cocoon of lava.

Bright yellow flames sprang to life and brought false daylight to the display vault. Within the opaque shadows of Lute's exhaust and the fumes of smelting marble stretched hideous wings. Eyes brighter than the sun, the color of melted ore, shone through the veil of smoggy darkness. They sized up the repurposed cathedral, the freedom, and what precisely to do with that freedom. And the dragon chose vengeance.

Head akin to a horse's in size, the dragon's triangular jaw unhinged and belched molten flame across the vault, the flames splashing across Zephyr's men with a wet slap. The screams only lasted for a few seconds before the flesh and bone beneath it melted. From skin to liquid, just like that. Terrifying, but so metal.

"Mandy!" Natalya's voice called over the roar of the beast, the din of chaos, and the instruments' clashing. I blinked away the afterimage of the bubbling flames just in time to see her sling Lute over her head in my direction. They twisted in the air, passing just in front of another cascade of dragonfire. I could have sworn that a drop or two of the smelting liquid actually *touched* Lute's strings, but the instrument did not burst alight. I dropped the battle-leg and tossed Natalya's lyre back to her. As the warm wood grain of the lyre left my right hand, my left caught and closed around the cool neck of Lute. Immediately, a flood of thoughts and emotions invaded my consciousness as the spirits of the instrument, the voices of the souls, greeted me.

"*Hello, old friend,*" they said. I smiled warmly before strumming a heavy, rejuvenating riff that ground against my eardrums. Twelve of Zephyr's thugs remained, frantically trying to dodge barrages of dragonfire and backfiring magical artifacts. Zephyr himself scrambled behind a pillar, clutching his longsword and sweating profusely. It was time to give the warlord a personal performance. Smoke dribbled from Lute's sound hole and strengthened to a torrent as I picked up the tempo. The notes became determined, then grueling, and finally ravenous. I bellowed the lyrics in Zephyr's direction.

**Blood boiling in retribution**
**Witness the smelting**
**Death on wings comes for you**

Lute's metalsmoke ravaged the pedestals carrying artifacts. Countless trinkets clattered to the ground. Some sprouted legs and waddled off on shaky feet. Others became invisible, tripping up the thugs as they scrabbled away from the dragon and the noise. Most simply erupted into fireballs of varying color. The inside of the display vault rapidly oscillated between dawn and midnight as the fireballs, dragon-fire, and tendrils of black smoke savagely collided. I strode forward through the carnage, carving a straight line. Natalya followed. The raw sound was on the right track, but I willed Lute to shift the tone even blacker.

**The seeds you reap**
**Rot in your hands**
**Buried in your misdeeds**
**Drowning in the sands**

The dragon's tattered wings flexed and swung in great arcs of battering wind. They launched the fleeing mercenaries absurdly far across the hall. The scaly wyrmling's small size—around twenty feet—did nothing to diminish its fearsomeness, and the liquid flames of its furious breath splattered along with the blood of its prey. I glimpsed Ord engaging one of the thugs, swiftly disarming and stabbing a man nearly three times his size with his own weapon. Only one adversary blocked my path to Zephyr.

"*He's not getting away,*" Lute said.

**The beast sets fire**
**To your lies**
**Beneath the flames**
**Lies a darkness that will never die**

With a flourish of my calloused and bloody fingers, the rivulets of smoke curling around me surged forward and struck into the guard, wrapping around his ankle. Another rip and bend of the strings whipped him toward the ceiling. His scream floated through the air until the dragon, fascinated by flying prey, pounced and caught him midair. Molten, glowing spittle dribbled out from the corners of the beast's jaws and over the now-limp body like juices over a roast pig. I made a mental note to write a song about that image.

Zephyr whimpered at my approach, crouching on his knees with wide eyes under his wider brow. Tears soaked his face. His shoulders slumped in defeat and terror.

**See my face**

I planted my feet in front of the warlord.

**And put out your eyes**

"Please," he wailed over the music. "I'll give you anything you want. Just please don't hurt me. You can have fame, you can have wealth, you can get on the king's court! Anything, just say the word." His begging and bargaining merged as I stopped strumming. All at once, my injuries resurged over the adrenaline, pinging different pain receptors in a mishmash succession.

I stood over him, a demon with singed clothing and savaged long hair. My face was now in a new paint pattern designed by dust, soot, and gore. Small rivulets of blood trickled from my tapered ears, and my hunched position—more from exhaustion than anything—resembled a wretched gargoyle ready to pounce.

"*We want Emile,*" Lute said.

Natalya, who looked so pristine that one couldn't have guessed she had just gone through a battle, crouched in front of her former manager. Her brow furrowed into a deadly serious line. "You're going to leave me be for good, do you hear me, Vossen? My instruments are *my* property, and you can expect worse than this if you ever try to take them again."

I inspected the ruined cathedral. Bodies strewn about, patches of marble floor melted away by broken artifacts, a discarded battle-leg, and a young dragon fervently climbing the wall toward the skylight. It was hard to imagine an outcome *worse* than this.

"You aren't going to continue exploiting people to gain wealth anymore, Zephyr. Your coasting is over," Natalya said firmly.

Zephyr sneered through his tears at my friend, "And what coattails are there to ride where you're concerned, Natalya? You churn out the fruits of unwarranted goodwill and fervor year after year, and simpletons still ravenously shovel the horseshit into their mouths. At least your instrument had some value, but what value is there in a whore who writes garbage about her lovers?"

Before Lute or I could step in, Natalya's fist crushed Zephyr's nose with a meaty crunch. The pig of a warlord squealed in agony, blood already gushing from his nostrils and gurgling in his open, wailing mouth. Behind us, Ord dragged the battle-leg behind him with bloodstained fingers. Brutal.

"Thought you might need this, my lady," the goblin grumbled. Natalya nodded appreciatively, bringing an even greater terror to the noble's eyes. She hefted the weighty limb and let it hover over Zephyr. Not a threat, a promise. Natalya met my eyes for a moment and motioned with her head for me to ask my questions. *Fuck, I'd almost forgotten.*

"How do I find your sadistic wizard friend Emile?" I said.

Zephyr's bloodshot and teary eyes narrowed at me, "What? Did he curse you or something, freak? Is that why you look like that?"

"He cursed a friend of mine, and he needs to atone for that," I replied stiffly.

I got a snicker in response, "So he cursed another of your freak friends. You choose to look like this all on your own?" A wheezing chuckle escaped his lips.

I crouched in front of the man, eyes hardening. All my life, I'd been called an aberration, cast out of everyday life because of my appearance or my music. But if being different from Zephyr made me a freak, so be it. The man had no one except for those he paid and his stolen treasures. "This freak wants to know where he can find Emile," I said.

The battle-leg crunched into the floor beside him, making him flinch and squeal. "All right! All right, I'll tell you where he is if you let me go," he blubbered. The leg deserved a song of its own with how useful it had been.

I nodded slowly.

"*Tell us*," Lute urged.

"I don't know where he is," Zephyr said, watching my eyebrows knit further, "*but* I know where he'll be in a couple months' time. He'll be at the king's ascension anniversary festival, here in Cloverhold."

"*Finally.*" I felt Lute's shudder of anticipation, of rage, and relief.

Natalya scratched her chin, "There's a contest of song that I'm meant to play at during the festival. King Kevan will be the judge, meaning it's likely that Emile will be there too. I'll get you as close as I can, Mandy," she said. The gratitude and resolve in her eyes softened my furrowed brow, but my pulse quickened at her smile.

"Metal," I said. I waited for Ord and Natalya's quizzical looks, but they both nodded in agreement.

Shattering glass and the tinkling of shards reaching the floor announced that the baby dragon had reached the skylight. Molten dribbles of its saliva trickled down the darkening walls like glowing, Hadean vines. This undeniably raw imagery didn't distract from the chief problem, however. It seemed that the dragon was intent on making this place its new nest, and that meant the climate within the stronghold would change drastically. No matter how deliciously infernal a man-made structure converted into a volcano sounded, it wouldn't be a place for us to stick around.

Ord seemed to glean the same thoughts from the situation. "We should go, my lady." Natalya nodded in agreement, and the four of us hobbled out of the ballroom, Natalya, Ord, Lute, and I.

"Wait! What about my house?" Zephyr wailed after us.

"Take it up with the dragon!" I called back. We strolled out of the burning stronghold, with the roars of the juvenile dragon and the furious screams of a poser echoing after us.

The trek out the front door of the Vossen Estate and out the gates was a quiet one. Natalya clutched her lyre to her like a mother to a newborn. Ord methodically cleaned gore and ash from his knives, and by the time we passed through the iron gates, the knives were the cleanest thing on his person.

Dawn hadn't quite graced the horizon when we took the last, exhausted step across the threshold of the Vossen Estate grounds, but the glowing of the keep brought a false sunrise to the area. My vision barely picked out the shadow of the dragon atop the structure, raining molten fire down upon it, making a new home. Natalya and Ord drew up their cowls.

"*Say something to her,*" Lute said suddenly.

"What?" I whispered, confusion scrawled across my face and anxiety constricting my chest.

"We should be going, Mandy," Natalya said. "This spectacle won't go on unnoticed, and it's better if I'm not here when prying eyes arrive." She smiled that comforting, genuine smile of hers. "I can't thank you enough for this. I mean that, truly."

My mouth vomited out words before she could walk away. "Natalya, it's not true, what Vossen said. You're not what he says you are. You're just doing what you love, and I hope you know that it never has to be more than that."

Lute didn't have a snarky response for that.

"I know, Mandy. And I hope you know the same. You're a good friend, and I'm glad you were with us tonight." She leaned in and her lips softly brushed my cheek. Raven curls tickled the shoulder of my coat. "Look for my message as the festival draws near, and I'll help the two of you take that son of a bitch down."

Lute hummed, "*Thank you, Natalya.*"

Ord patted my arm. The same spot where his skull had cracked me, but I ignored the brightening pain. "We'll see you soon, son," he said.

As the bardess and the goblin slinked away, I grinned and waved slyly. Natalya broke into another smile as she called out, "I think I know the title of my next song: The Dragon and the Death Metal Bard." They disappeared into the night, leaving Lute and I alone.

For a moment, we simply basked in the artificial dawn of the burning stronghold. Groundskeepers and mercenaries alike stood awestruck along the vast gardens, mouths agape as the dragon continued to howl and rend the roof apart. Zephyr Vossen's mournful wails joined the beast in harmony as his men trawled him from the flaming structure and onto the grass. Twisting streams of magma slowly dissolved the walls, a stone candle melting in front of our eyes. Now that we weren't at risk of liquefying with the rest of the fortress, the warm glow of the blaze made my eyes droop, far enough away to be like a soothing campfire.

"Think the *Troll's Head* has any rooms available?" I asked.

"*Likely. Did you see how empty the place was?*" Lute said.

I nodded but kept my transfixed eyes on the dragon, perched on the reclaimed home that had once been its prison.

Lute paused for a moment before speaking again, "I'm *glad you're alive.*"

"You too," I said with a smile. "After all, we still have a wizard to hunt."

# WIZARD PUNCHER

# Wizard Puncher

Lute and I stalked through the milling crowd, scanning for our prey. Drinking garbage whiskey and vomiting up subpar food had proven to be a less than worthwhile pastime, and the Ascension Festival had been crawling along since dawn. With my normal activities of drinking and avoiding people becoming too monotonous, Lute and I decided to camouflage ourselves in the crowd until Emile showed his despicable face.

Blending in was only possible due to the sheer number of citizens that milled about between performances on the different stages. Four different grandstands surrounded a decent-sized lake, a water-filled crater in the vague shape of a dragon. Apparently, it was in this very spot that King Kevan and his compatriots had slain the beast and solidified his rise to the throne. The different stages were named after his old adventuring party. To honor the historic date, the king threw a massive music festival each year on the day.

*"You would have a better view of the place from a stage,"* Lute grumbled. They jostled as a man collided with my shoulder and continued his unobservant rush to the Drachmir Stage. Lute was strapped loosely to my back, and I felt each spirit within the instrument squirming in anticipation to unleash

their rage. The dark scorch mark from the Dragonfire re-mained, but they expressed no discomfort from it.

I sighed. "Natalya was lucky enough to get us a pass to the sovereign seating area. It's the place that the king is sitting, and I can all but guarantee that Emile will be there too."

"*If he shows up at all.*"

I silently prayed to the metal gods that he would. If Emile didn't show, it was back to square one, and our efforts to find him—just shy of a year—would be a complete waste of time. That was too brutal of a thought to entertain.

My new boots squished and sifted through mud that smelled suspiciously like urine. I glanced up the small but noticeable slope to the latrine area and cursed whatever idiot had designated the spot there. The piss dribbled down the dusty slant, slowly enveloping the sparse grass and dry, packed soil of the festival grounds like a foul-smelling grave-yard. I groaned and hurried out of the urine swamp as quickly as I could while dragging my feet on any dry grass I could find. Subdued fairgoers sat amid the grimy hillsides and waited for the next show to begin. Their blank eyes whispered of dehydration and exhaustion, no doubt the toll of being in the sun all day without a waterskin. Luckily, the sun was currently smothered by a flock of billowing clouds.

Despite the piss bog getting on my nerves, I relished the sights and sounds of the festival. Vendors peddled inex-pensive cuisine for criminally high prices, and the biggest performers of the day had entire tents selling garments and trinkets on their behalf. Empty ale mugs littered the uneven ground for passersby to pick up with the promise that turn-ing in mugs would net them a free drink. Varied bouquets of dried sweat, greasy food, cheap ale, an assortment of different smokes and vomit rushed my nostrils. Excited voices bickered over who was the best performer at the festival, when the king would show up, who Natalya Promptua was dating. I admit that my ears perked up at the mention of her name, but the current of the sentient ocean of passersby washed the conversation away.

"*Some of us remember this place,*" Lute hummed.

I cocked my head as I rounded the lake and headed to the Sovereign Stage, the main stage for the celebration. "You went to the Ascension Festival?"

"*A few of us. In our lives, we did many things. Remembering this, it feels...good.*"

"And Emile took those lives away from you," I said, my brow darkening.

"*He did.*" They stayed silent after that for a few minutes. Even after hearing this countless times, my head still burned in fury each time I thought about it. For some reason I could not fathom, Emile had ripped people from their lives with shadow magic and trapped them in a surreal prison of strings and wood. No one should be allowed to do that, and the terrifying question was whether the king knew about Emile's exploits or even *sanctioned* them.

Well, Emile would have Lute and I to deal with today either way. My coat, tastefully faded from the battle against Zephyr Vossen, billowed behind me and brushed shoulders and torsos in the maze of milling people. Ink from a recent dye session rubbed off on them, unnoticed for now. My corpsepaint was more raw than ever, with jagged shapes resembling vines spreading from the dark voids that were my eyes and mouth.

I'd finally managed to slick my black hair behind my pointed ears despite its length.

The newest addition to my persona was a twisting web of tattooed ink that spanned the length of my forearms. I'd begrudgingly accepted Lute's suggestions and included the most metal sights from our time together. The Birchward's trees, behemoth toads, a shapeshifter ghoul, crows, and a slavering baby dragon. Together, they wove a hellish tapestry of woe and mayhem across my arms, and the rolled-up sleeves of my coat left ink stains on my wrists that resembled clouds of dark smoke. A pitch-black appearance if I'd ever seen one; a vengeful angel that had crawled from the abyss just for this occasion.

The Sovereign Stage towered over the gathering crowd in the late afternoon sun in a monstrous obelisk. Massive braziers affixed to the structure lit the stage, perfectly illuminating the performer and somehow stealing light from the rest of the surrounding space. Before long, the sun would plummet to embrace the horizon and all that existed would be the performer on the stage. Deep envy gurgled in my stomach at the thought of other bards getting the opportunity to showcase their music at this venue. Or perhaps it was just more bile from my last dismal meal.

Gentle, crooning melodies drifted from the stage as the current act, a man by the name of Edvard Reeshan, sang whispered pillowtalk to an audience of thousands. Humans, elves, and goblins stood reverently silent, drinking the sweet mead of his rhythm. I focused my ears past his alluring lyrics and marveled at his technical skill. His fingers worked with the flourish of an artisan, pulling together and blending chords from what felt like different dimensions entirely to create a folk tone that shivered the ears.

*"There's the Sovereign Seating area, where the king will be,"* Lute's voice interjected. I shook my head free of Reeshan's seductive chorus and snaked through the raucous crowd toward an unnecessarily tall seating tower constructed of lacquered wood and steel supports. Palace guards oversaw every inch of the structure, with more on each level as the spire climbed higher into the heavens. I searched my breast pocket and fished out a folded square of parchment. Natalya had given it to me a few days prior, explaining that it was a written pass for me and Lute to gain access to the scaffold. Actually, it had been Ord who had given it to me, explaining that Natalya was laying low before the festival since she was the headliner. While I understood completely, it didn't wash away the disappointment of not seeing her again.

I glanced down at the parchment. "Fuck me," I said. The papyrus was completely stained through by black ink. No writing was discernible on the now soggy-with-pigment leaflet that was my ticket to getting within reach of our quarry. This was brutal.

"WHY WOULD YOU DO THAT?" Lute screamed in my mind's ear. *"We needed that to get in!"*

"Hold on," I said. My mind scrambled to solve this blunder, but nothing came after Lute's dizzying barrage of frustrated wails stunned my brain. All that echoed through my mind was my own thoughts and Lute's cursing me out. "What if we found Natalya and asked her to write another one?"

*"You think we can just stroll through a crowd of thousands to the stage, walk backstage without being stopped, and then*

*find Natalya right before she plays the biggest show of her life?"* Lute fumed.

"I don't know! Fuck, what do we do?" My one-way conversation with Lute was starting to draw attention. I looked around wildly, searching for something that could help us, but was met with only confused and concerned stares. I could do nothing. The guards wouldn't take kindly to us storming the seating tower, and there was no guarantee that we could find Natalya in time to write us another pass.

Rapid pops and a shower of colorful fireworks arced from the stage's apex, signifying the conclusion of Edvard Reeshan's set. But to Lute and I, it was the painful gong announcing our ticking clock. Green and blue sparks rained from the darkening sky like molten droplets of starlight before fizzling out some thirty feet above the crowd. If we were going to reach the Sovereign Stage, now would be the chance.

"Citizens of Enotia! Please welcome the Slayer of Kaan Superior, the Piper King, the Everyman Ruler...King Kevan the First!" a voice boomed overhead. Another rapid crackle of purple fireworks detonated over the top of the stage, lighting up the now indigo stratosphere. The braziers took on the same violet hue and illuminated a group of figures as they emerged from backstage. Though I was over three-hundred feet from the grandstand, the polished glint of the king's crown was unmistakable. Beside him prowled multiple guards, and a son of a bitch with stringy, pale hair.

"*That's him. He's here!*" Lute roared.

Dread flowed coldly in my bloodstream as I considered our choices. One, rush the stage and likely be killed by the king's overzealous guards and their crossbows—or Emile. Two, wait for Emile and the king to approach the seating tower and likely be killed by the king's overzealous guard with their longswords—or Emile.

After weighing those options, I began clawing my way through the throng of oblivious passersby, knocking food or ale from hand and ignoring indignant protests. Emile was here, in our grasp, and he would not be getting away. If we took to the stage, Lute and I could get within a perfect striking distance. The stunt could backfire horribly, but it would be our best chance.

Deeper into the ocean of onlookers, the pressure and density became greater, slowing our movement. A trail of ink-stained shoulders was left in my wake through the mob. There eventually came a point where I could swim no further, some fifty feet from the stage where the brutal pressure throttled my frame and squeezed my eyeballs. My head began to ache. I glowered through my corpsepaint at the grandstand and watched Emile skulk across stage left while the king bathed in the people's admiration.

The wizard looked unremarkable, much more akin to a slimy merchant or businessman than a mage. His well-tailored trousers and vest fit his slim figure well, and he had foregone the stereotypical robes for a lengthy maroon tailcoat embroidered with silvery trim. A pale-green pendant hung from his neck on a thin chain. His sense of style was vastly different from what I had expected, but I would never mistake the sinister smirk on his thin face, nor the yellow eyes that belonged in the skull of a smug cobra.

Rage burned behind my eyes, and I felt Lute grow hotter against my back. We were right in front of him, and the bastard didn't even see us. I had expected him to notice us, to pick us out of the crowd and squint in anger or fear. But he did none of those things. Unless we got the people around us to move, we would be doomed to scowl uselessly at the wizard from afar.

Someone's hair flitted in front of my face, and I lost Emile for the scariest of moments. The dark follicles were tied tightly into a tail and trailing from the scalp of a well-dressed countryman.

"Loukus!" I shouted into the back of his head.

The noble of Moashanda whipped his head around in surprise, smacking my face again with his ponytail. His eyes widened at the sight of me, and a subdued smile broke across his stoic face. "Well met, Ozzymandias! Music brings our paths together again."

I sidestepped his greeting. "Loukus, I have to get to the stage. It's an emergency." Normally, a familiar face in a concert crowd would have been the highlight of my day, but our grasp on opportunity was slipping. Luckily, the stern commitment on Loukus's face returned, and he nodded curtly.

"*How is he going to manage this?*" Lute asked.

Without warning, Loukus shoved the elf in front of him, creating a sprawling chain of unbalance that brought everyone for twelve feet ahead to the dusty, trampled ground. Given the precariousness of people craning forward to get a glimpse of the king, he hadn't needed to push with much force. The village noble then ripped the sword from his belt with a metallic screech.

That shriek of metal against its scabbard infected the crowd with a viral terror, spasming their limbs and glazing their wide, terrified eyes with milky blindness. However, only citizens within a certain distance heard him. The rest chanted Kevan's name in a fervor.

"Make way!" Loukus's voice was drowned in the clamors of admiration for the king.

"*He isn't making enough noise,*" Lute urged. "*But he's getting some attention.*" I wasn't sure that I liked the tone in which Lute said those words. Searching with wild eyes, my gaze finally landed on a pair of royal kingsguard shoving through the mob of countryfolk toward Loukus. Concert security ready to deliver a troublemaker from the premises. Lute was right; all the nobleman was doing was getting himself and possibly both of us thrown out, and he still hadn't cleared an adequate path to the stage.

My mind raced and finally landed on a solution, albeit a slap-dash one. Lute and I could make the noise we needed to clear a path to the stage, but any chance of us getting the jump on Emile would no longer be an option. As I yanked Lute from my back and hefted their gouged wooden frame in my arms, I felt their assent. There was no going back, but my friend and I were finally face to face with the monster that had imprisoned innocent souls in a soulless chamber. There would not be another opportunity like this again.

And we would make sure that we took this full opportunity for justice. Raw, brutal, pitch-black justice.

The necrotic explosion of squealing, scratching distortion immediately silenced the crowd, suffocating all other sound in a sheet of stunned terror. The kingsguard approaching our position clapped their gauntleted palms over their ears, and every citizen's eyes shot to me, trying to comprehend what was in their midst. Standing amongst them was a demon elf dressed like death, with a black-and-white face of scowling focus, a lute the color of fresh blood, and raven smoke curling off him. King Kevan took a wary step back, even from the relative safety and distance of the stage. The man's bushy black beard didn't hide the confused grimace, and the crown upon his brow pushed his eyebrows even further together as he squinted at me.

But the face my gaze locked onto was that of the king's mage. Emile's cheeks had become a similar color to a bleached skull. His nostrils flared in anger, or possibly embarrassment, at the prospect of seeing his old experiment confronting him. But what I noticed above all were his serpent's eyes growing dark with hatred and fear, an apex predator that had wandered too far in its hubris and finally discovered a threat.

"*That's right, motherfucker*," Lute growled, "*we're still here.*"

I didn't waste any time in capitalizing on our stolen attention, throwing my voice in the scariest growl possible while still trying to keep it legible to the ears. "Emile Gurren! I've come to avenge your misdeeds and the innocents you've tormented."

Hushed and quizzical murmurs rippled throughout the crowd, but quickly quieted as the king called back out to me. "And who are you, stranger, who brings this accusation?" Kevan demanded. His voice, while projecting with the confidence and range of a practiced orator, could not match mine.

As I opened my mouth to speak, a clear, familiar voice shouted from behind the king. "His name is Ozzymandias, the Death Metal Bard and a good friend. Hear him, your grace. He speaks the truth." A smile touched my lips as Natalya and Ord emerged from the back of the stage, drawing gasps and a few confused ripples of applause. She was draped in a beautiful vermillion dress with bare shoulders and a short train behind her. Ord wore his same leather jerkin with sewn-in knife sheaths. Their eyes met mine and they nodded as one. My smile widened, drawing horrified whimpers from the cowering citizens nearest me.

My gaze hardened as I leveled it back at Emile. The wizard glared at Natalya and Ord before meeting my eyes again. However, I quickly realized that it wasn't me he was looking at. He was staring with loathing at Lute. A black hatred stirred in my chest like a boiling vat of ink. This monster showed no reflection, no remorse—only disdain and anger that one of his past experiments had dared to show itself again.

"You took the souls from ordinary people, Emile. You used Shadow Magic to bind them into an inanimate form, trapped them in this instrument. This prison of strings you've used to house these stolen spirits returns to haunt you. Death Metal has given them the means for vengeance, and they will take it today!" I yelled at the stage. Without realizing, I had been taking inevitable steps through the crowd—now parting like a tear in parchment—and toward the stage. Confused looks at the term "Death Metal" rippled across the faces nearest me.

Emile stood solid and straight-backed, eyes narrowed and unwavering from Lute and I as we drew nearer. His shoulders were hunched like a rabbit ready to bolt, but his lips stayed firmly pressed together in a grim line.

King Kevan scratched his beard worriedly, feeling the air as it stilled further and further, anticipating a storm. "Emile, do you know this elf?" the king asked.

The wizard shook his head slowly, speaking slowly in a voice that resembled a snake made of silk. "Not in the slightest, your grace. I haven't the faintest clue what this ghoul is accusing me of."

"*Liar!*" Lute screamed. I watched Emile's eyes twitch slightly as if he could hear them. It appeared that none around us could, however.

Natalya strode beside the king and laid a steadying hand on his shoulder. "I can vouch for Mandy, your grace. He's a good man, and he would not be trying to deceive us. I believe him, wholeheartedly and truly."

Despite my rising adrenaline and anger, my cheeks grew pleasantly hot at her defense of me. I felt Lute shaking in my hands.

"I believe him too!" Loukus shouted from behind me. "This elf saved my village."

"You do not seriously believe this, do you?" Emile looked sidelong at the king. His entire posture had relaxed after the initial shock.

"Whomever this elf claims to be, he seems touched in the head or influenced by some sinister being. Just look at him—the very image of a demon looking to terrorize a peaceful kingdom."

*Metal,* I thought. *What a compliment.*

The crowd murmured at Emile's lies, unsure of who to believe. The king's mage was a high position in the Enotian ruling class, and challenging the person who held that station was not done lightly.

Lute's voice surged in my mind, making my blinking eyes widen along with Emile's and Natalya's. *"Let us speak."*

Without thinking or asking what they meant, I raised my hand above my head and let it hang there for a fraction of a second. I saw Emile mouth the word "No" before I threw my arm down and hammered my fingers against Lute's strings hard enough to draw blood.

The necrotic grumble of Lute's tone became darkly deafening, registering so low that only elf ears would have been able to hear the note. Instead, the crowd around me felt the shockwave of the chord bounce and rattle in their ribcages. Hands tightened over ears and screams erupted throughout the throng of people, but their screams dwindled to nothing when in competition with Lute's.

Flames, smoke, and deathly cries accompanied the abyssal sound of the instrument. Sparks and embers floated within the billowing metalsmoke along with the mournful impressions of faces. They writhed and twisted, calling in the voices of men, women, and children; and elves, humans, and goblins alike. Finally, they used the individual voices of those who Emile had doomed to an eternity of confinement into a single body with nothing but the screaming remnants of strangers for company or comfort. It was the first time that something metal had ever made me sick. Death Metal shouldn't be used like that, to bring about the suffering of innocents.

The souls that resided within Lute screamed and hurled abuse at Emile, one after the other, over and over.

"Monster!" one bellowed.

"Soul-stealer!" another screamed.

"Betrayer!"

"Murderer!"

Amid the inferno that boiled from Lute, the furious face of a woman rippled to the top and casted a guttural scream over the festival grounds, "I trusted you! *I trusted you!*" Emile's face paled to near translucency at the sight of her. "Every word from your mouth, lies. Filth! Liar! Wretch!" she screamed.

Kevan's face morphed between mourning and indignant rage, "Quelenna!" His shouts were lost within the howl of Death Metal and spirits wailing their loathing at the wizard beside him. Gasps rippled outward in the crowd who had been close enough to hear. Kevan's guards drew their swords in a symphony of ringing metal and leveled them at the wizard.

*I recognize that name.* She'd been the woman from the missing flyers at the *Troll's Head Tavern.*

Trapped within Lute was one of the King's closest friends, an elf who had disappeared more than a year ago and thought dead.

"I trusted you!" Quelenna's words washed over the festival grounds for miles in every direction. They glided over the lake where the slain dragon still presumably rested, and they soared into the heavens, spreading word of Emile's misdeeds to the stars. The wizard himself had settled into a silent, seething rage that radiated from his well-dressed form in a visible aura. His hands clenched and unclenched, and his jaw tightened with enough force that it looked like it might implode. King Kevan, Natalya, Ord, Loukus, and the entire crowd leveled their gaze at the king's mage, waiting for a sputtering explanation, but none came. Instead, my eyes caught his left hand moving from his side, raising slowly...

Immediately, Lute and I broke into a paralyzing blastbeat, sending a rapid-fire wave of drop-tuned notes that punctured the skin and immobilized the muscles. Elves, humans, and goblins froze in terror as the sound chased the air from their lungs. Emile gulped at the acrid, smoky air like a fish and brought his hand up further. I willed the tendrils of smoke to rush from me in inky coils, constricting around the wizard's wrist. While the gas twisted his arm behind his back, I sprinted through the now-large opening in the crowd toward the stage, still furiously strumming the riff.

"*Whatever you do, don't let him touch you,*" Lute urged. "*That's how he got us.*"

"Keep the mage at arm's length—you make it sound so easy."

Onstage, Emile bucked against the shadowy restraint, gray teeth snarling in a lizard's grimace. His tailcoat billowed behind him, and his long hair blew backward with every thumping beat of the riff. The audience, finally able to regain their breath, writhed before the stage in a screaming cascade. I allowed the tendrils to slingshot me forward and soar through the air until my muddy boots clomped down onto the stage. My lower throat already warm and pulpy, I loosed a gangrenous scream in the words that Lute and I had written specifically for the villainous wizard.

**An evil lord, despair**

**Sweat the blood of your victims**

Emile ripped his hand from the metal's smoky grasp and flung it forward. Splinters of timber and jagged shards of iron tore themselves from the stage behind him and rocketed toward me in a deadly hailstorm. With a gruesome lick on Lute's strings and an unearthly grunt, I cast the debris aside. The wood and ore ripped the canopy of the grandstand off its foundations and flung it into the lake with a monumental splash. A nasty bruise had already blossomed on Emile's wrist like a black orchid.

**Their vengeance rends your flesh**
**Lashing, tearing, peeling**
**Bleeding you bare**

The tentacles of Death Metal fumes rushed for the wizard again, but he brought his hands together in a resounding clap. A deluge of frigid magic danced from his fingertips and froze the tendrils solid. Another clap and they shattered into fragments of midnight ice. He glanced up and met my eyes with a smug smirk.

"*Don't let up!*" Lute said. "*We have to wear him down!*" That was all well and simple, but Lute and I could only keep this up for so long. Eventually, I would tire, and if Emile kept up his stamina longer than me, I would be pulverized to dust. Or have my soul stolen. *Or both.* Brutal.

A bright flash drew my attention to the mage's right hand as a small, glowing orb materialized between his middle and ring fingers. Faster than my eye could blink, Emile hurled the orb in my direction. The tiny projectile crossed the twenty feet between us with lightning speed, and my eyes finally refocused and saw it before it crashed into my forehead.

Light, sharp and terrible, overtook my vision when the orb exploded and expanded into a green supernova. Lute and I were flung backward in flames, and the music was silenced like a knife hacking off a limb. The king's guards weren't fortunate enough to dive out of the way and were vaporized, charred viscera pattering dryly onto the ground in strips of guard-jerky. The smell was awful.

We came to a splintery halt near stage right, barely avoiding rolling off the side of the grandstand altogether. Pricks of timber stuck from my face in a bizarre hybrid of a skunk and a porcupine. I gulped as the air helplessly banished from my lungs. Natalya and Ord scrambled to my side while the king gawped in disbelief and horror at his mage.

"Just breathe, Mandy," Natalya said. "You're going to be okay." Her eyes told a slightly more urgent tale, and Ord scratched his head with the butt of a knife as if contemplating how I proposed to walk away from this fight alive.

Blood trickled down from my hairline, adding a fresh red streak to my face paint. I had to admit between groans that bloody corpsepaint was obscenely metal.

Emile's polished gray boots clacked confidently across the shredded stage, kicking stray planks and bolts from his path. The tailcoat began to flap in wind that wasn't coming from the usual direction, and the wizard raised his hands to either side of him. "How did you command the vessel? What trickery did you use? You'll tell me, and then you'll pay dearly for using Quelenna against me. I loved her!"

I wheezed on thin air, finally filling my lungs after what felt like a full minute of gasping for oxygen. "And what a shit way to show her how much you care." I tried and failed to sit up, still clutching Lute's neck firmly.

"What in the Kaans is wrong with you, Emile?" King Kevan demanded. "You know what Shadow Magic does. It corrupts and twists everything it touches. It's forbidden!"

The wizard tapped his temple with his middle fingernail. "Ah, but within it lies infinite possibility. The soul holds more power than any known force in the cosmos, and Shadow Magic is the only way to harness it." His fingers brushed the hair from his eyes. "Do you wish to bend to the mercy of the Kaans? Are you content with the floods that ravage the Easterlands or the giants that patrol the north, hmm? The way forward is through shadow magic. Greatness can't be discovered until we are willing to level with being monstrous, until we stare our fiendish desires in the face and extend a hand. This instrument is the key, and I'll be needing it back to continue my work."

*"It can't end. You can't let him take us,"* Lute begged. I could say nothing. I could *do* nothing but stare through blurry, concussed eyes at Emile's venomous smirk. I closed them to stop the world from spinning and to hide my fear.

Emile's howl of agony ripped my eyes back open. It was a screeching, tooth-breaking sound that I would never have expected from a person of that stature. The wizard stumbled and clutched his now-red hand. Blood gushed from his wrist where a white-feathered arrow had pierced the flesh, and his arm flopped numbly like a limp eel as he swore and cursed and spat. Emile's eyes widened as he roared in a fury at something behind me.

"Up we go, Mandy." The voice of a friend spoke in my ear as a strong pair of arms hooked underneath my tattooed arms. My shaky eyes registered Patch smiling down at me. The farmboy hoisted me to my feet as if I were no more than a sack of grain, steadying me with a reassuring grin. His beard had grown in significantly more, and his hair was tied back in a tail. But he was still the same bright-eyed lad I'd braved the Birchward with. "How do you know Natalya Promptua? She's our absolute favorite!" he whispered.

"Long story," Natalya said through a relieved smile, still kneeling by my side.

Korinne appeared from behind us, brandishing her long-bow and a quiver bursting with arrows. She glanced at Patch with the gleaming eyes of a vindicated wife. "Still think it wasn't a good idea for me to bring my bow?"

Tears threatened to overtake my already muddled vision and wash away my face paint. My friends, spread far across this land before this festival, were here for me and Lute. My appearance, my music, my bond with Lute; none of it mattered to them, and they were here to help a friend in trouble. A tear finally slipped from the corner of my eye and carved down my cheek. Brutal.

"You short-sighted, vile little insects!" Emile cursed as he snapped the shaft off the arrow, leaving the head still buried deep in his bleeding forearm. The wizard's eyes were wild with bloodlust, and he leveled an accusatory finger at the cluster of people who stood in the way of his ambition. "You can't see it, can you? The world that I can create with shadow magic could be a paradise!"

I hoisted Lute into my arms and set my fingers ready for another round, "The spirits you destroy can't be worth that, Emile. No more souls for you." I gritted my teeth and felt my feet solidify beneath me. Smoke poured from my body and coagulated into sharp tendrils, itching for violence.

I felt Natalya tense next to me, her own instrument in her hands. Ord and Patch drew their respective blades, and Korinne nocked another arrow and nodded curtly. Even King Kevan unsheathed his ceremonial blade and stood beside us. His crown was askew and his beard singed, but his dark eyebrows knit together in regal rage.

Emile sighed and rubbed his bloody thumb and forefinger along his pale eyebrows. With a flick of his other hand, the back of the Sovereign Stage blew apart into matchsticks, leaving just the flat platform. Behind the stage, the drag-on-crater-lake rippled and boiled in a dark blue stew.

"I knew that there would be a day when I'd have to put you in your place, Kevan," Emile said. "You know that you couldn't have prevailed that day without me, right? All of those people that you led to their deaths, resting beside the bones of the beast at the bottom of that crater. It was with my help that you even left that battle alive." A disturbing emerald glow emanated deep under the lake's surface.

"*Bones of the Beast. Good song title*," Lute said.

"Not the time, but yes," I nodded.

The restless pool frothed higher, clawing further up the shore and no more than twenty feet from the back of the stage. My gaze was drawn to slimy, skeletal hands wrenching themselves from the watery grip of the battle-made lake. Dozens, and then hundreds of waterlogged skulls emerged from the depths, bobbing like necrotic apples in a barrel. Eye sockets brimming with algae swallowed any remaining radiance in the fading twilight, trained directly on me and my friends. Slimy helmets adorned some heads. Some skulls crumbled inward upon their exposure to air as their ashen foundations discovered a lack of integrity. Soot crept across the surface of the pool, freshly disturbed for the first time in nearly a decade. Even from more than two-hundred yards away, a deep, sulfuric smell rushed up my nostrils.

"By the Gods," Kevan gasped, and the previously writhing crowd stiffened in dreadful silence. Just one glance at the faces of Enotia citizens, and it was clear to see their terror, their fear that any movement would identify them as prey for the menacing wraiths that waded just a short distance away.

Emile's foxlike smile brought the hairs on my arms standing to a point. He shook his head slowly, eyes never leaving mine. "I'll take repossession of my property now, with or without your cooperation," he said. Ambition glimmered in his previously shadowed eyes.

"Eat shit, wizard," I smirked back. The next note that I blasted forth from Lute was like a heavily distorted gong, triggering a flurry of movement from the others onstage. Kevan and Patch rushed the mage, their swords held high. As I registered Emile's hands rising to counter them, I broke into a riff that crunched against the eardrum. Rhythmic, black bars punched the atmosphere in every direction, and the tentacles of midnight smog pummeled Emile. The disgraced mage staggered backward, bruising immediately and barely sidestepping furious swipes from the king and the farmboy. An arrow from Korinne whizzed past his ear by an inch. I found my voice as Natalya plucked discordant notes to compliment my verse.

**Arcane malefactor**

**Your deeds bleed**
**Behind your eyes**

The Death Metal fumes grew sharper, countless scorpion barbs stabbing hungrily for Emile. Ord leapt for the wizard, knives gripped tightly in each hand. Lithe as an eel, Emile raised his hand. The appendage extended into a viper and lunged forward to wrap around the goblin's throat. Ord stabbed at the scaly tentacle ferociously in an attempt to break free.

In the distance, the ripples of the lake grew with the shuffling advances of the undead. Emile only had to hold us off long enough for his hastily assembled army to take care of us.

Emile grunted and slung Ord into the surface of the stage. The bodyguard wheezed as all air was banished from his chest and his knives went pinwheeling from his grasp. Kevan and Patch rolled hastily to the side as Emile whipped his snake-arm in a viscous arc.

**Rivulets of death**
**Torrents of despair**

"He's *shrugging off everything we send at him,*" Lute snarled. We willed the tone to morph into something darker; heavier. Every note was a sweeping blade, the percussion behind the riff a pounding club. Natalya's accenting notes needled alongside the song, darts shooting into the chaotic storm of vengeful savagery that poured relentlessly from our performance.

All the while, Emile used every trick in his magician's toolkit to evade, brush aside, or slam through our attacks. Flames erupted from his palms in scalding shields; Korinne's arrows were simply engulfed in vision-bending singularities that materialized with a click of his fingers. Every wave of his gaunt hands crushed the splintery surface of the stage where Patch, Ord, or the king had barely dodged from. None of his terrifyingly dispassionate displays of power were enough to tear his eyes from me and Lute. The ambition to reclaim the instrument he had freely abandoned blazed behind his pupils. Now that he knew the power within the instrument could be tamed, he was another step closer to perfecting shadow magic.

Lute's emotions had been in tune with mine for nearly a year, but I felt them wash anew through me in a clear indication that they would never submit to the demands of their tormentor or anyone else. Despite their imprisonment, Death Metal had set them free.

**Your hands**
**Tainted by the whips of ambition**
**We take from you**
**And gouge your eyes**
**With the selfish fingers**

The sloshing of disjointed and uncoordinated undead steps drew nearer, and Emile still had not gone down. Our merry band was simultaneously stretched too thin and squeezed too tightly, about to be overwhelmed by both a horde of ghouls as well as the slimy mage who had conjured it. Death Metal clashed with the moans of the soulless husks. The incessant wailing and gurgling assaulted my ears.

"*The crowd,*" Lute urged. Somehow, their voice sounded smaller in my head with the stacked zombified choir vocalizing.

"What?" I yelled.

"*Get them involved! Remember Moashanda,*" My gaze swung wildly toward the other side of the stage where hundreds still remained, pale and terrified. The horror of the situation had sunk its teeth into the citizens of Enotia, and they were paralyzed by the venom. Many more were in the midst of fleeing.

But I saw a few heads bobbing. A few feet tapping. It was enough. Using every fiber of my pulpy vocal cords, I tore my attention away from Emile for a few precious seconds to address the crowd, holding against hope that my friends could hold their own without my sole focus on the mage. Their wide eyes snapped to me as I screamed.

"I want to see the biggest, most brutal pit that Enotia has ever seen, do you hear me? This is your night, your moment, your chance to use the rage you feel as one voice!"

Some of the shocked faces furrowed in determination; others still gaped disbelievingly at the approaching wraiths. Still more who were fleeing slowed to the beckoning scream. "I don't care if it's rage at someone you know, something in your life, or if you're just angry and you can't fathom why. You have a right to own your wrath—to give in to it. Take it out on this wizard and his army. Open up this *fucking pit!*" I shrieked.

One by one, the faces in the audience rippled and contorted. Their fear melted and bubbled over into fury. Even those in the midst of fleeing slowly lined up at the back of a Death Metal Battalion. All at once, their howls joined mine as I thrashed out a new riff. The rumble of thousands of feet mirrored the blazing percussion of the performance. With Loukus at their head, the crowd swarmed to either side of the stage like enraged hornets and engaged Emile's undead army.

**We are the hammer**
**That crushes the world**
**Blood oceans**
**Flooding salted fields**

Natalya screamed along with me, somehow anticipating the lyrics that Lute and I wrote in real time. A flurry of limbs both living and dead collided all around us; a sea of violence. And the rhythm of the mosh pit tide rose and fell with the undulating, crushing Death Metal. Loukus cut down a ghoul with his sword. One man tore a limb from a wraith and began using it as a slimy, sinewy club. A screaming young woman caved in a skull with a mallet, sending the undead assailant sprawling backward with a hammer-smashed face. Hair windmilled in time with the flurrying tempo, slapping ghouls across the brow before they were dismembered by the frenzied masses.

Across the stage, Emile bellowed in frustration and shoved his hand outward. Some wall of invisible force slammed against Patch, Ord, and the king and sent them tumbling from the stage and into the battle below. I lost sight of all three in the slurry of battle. Korinne's shout of alarm was followed swiftly by the twang of her bow. Her arrow collided with Emile's energy wall with a deep *whump*. It stayed stuck in the shield, appearing to hang in the air as the mage drew closer, gaining momentum. With another flick of his fingers, Korinne sailed into the writhing chaos below. My disbelieving eyes watched her stark white hair disappear between two blurry shapes on the battlefield. Natalya, Lute, and I faced down the wizard alone. Below us, the pit frothed with slime and blood and screams and blades. Nothing was discernible, only havoc.

Still, we played.

**The reckoning**

**Of our furious silence**

**Bursts forth and falls**

**On your head**

Spears of smoke, sharpened to a supernaturally fine point, lunged for Emile, only to be deflected by his shielding spell. Natalya scooped up one of Ord's discarded knives and hurled it at the bastard. It bounced off and clattered away.

"Give me. The lute," Emile growled, no more than ten feet from us.

"Never," Natalya said. I let my raspy howls fill up the atmosphere, staring directly into Emile's enraged face. He reached forward, hand blossoming in harsh white light, a sinister radiance.

**We shatter your bones**

**Spit on your desire**

**You are the nail**

**We are the hammer**

The moment his glowing hand connected with me and Lute's shadowy aura, my eyes were overwhelmed with a cacophony of purple explosions. They bled through my clenched eyelids and washed over and over in a riptide that refused to release me. I felt nothing; only the furious, rapid coursing of energy while Lute's raw tone echoed in my bleeding eardrums.

When I opened my eyes, feeling returned to my limbs, and I jolted upon the realization that I was no longer touching the stage. In fact, my body was twisting, spiraling upward after having been launched from the grandstand by the expense of power. Some hundred feet away, Natalya flailed in the air, her parabolic arc taking her further and further away. My coat flapped wildly around me like a pair of broken raven wings, and my hair danced in every conceivable random direction.

"*Don't stop playing!*" Lute's scream was barely heard over the rushing current in my ears. The air around me enveloped me in a roaring wind tunnel, sapping almost any other sensations except for the cool wood of Lute's neck and the worn gut of their strings. I still held the instrument. A weak wisp of black smoke trailed from the crimson body.

Emile's form hovered and drifted in the air above us, a misty halo emanating from his wind-tossed coat. It held him aloft among the clouds, a thunder god at twilight taunting us in front of the ethereal, ghostly moon. He'd hurled us into the air and then followed just to taunt us.

It was this image of the wizard that burned into my vision as Lute and I reached the peak of our trajectory. As quickly as we had risen, we began to plummet downward toward the craterlake. The massive body of water that now appeared no bigger than a puddle.

"PLAY!" Lute bellowed again. But the words were snatched from my mind as the ground blasted upward to greet us. So this was how I would go out: dropped from the sky by a homicidal mage.

Had to admit though, it was better than starving to death on the road. At the very least, I had a friend with me.

Between the gusts of wind that buffeted my eyes and all but peeled the paint from my face, my watery vision picked out a tumbling speck amid the dark and indifferent clouds. Natalya. She'd been blown into the sky with me.

"*We can find a way through this, you just have to play, Mandy!*"

My fingers battled against the resisting air, crawling inch by inch until they finally rested on Lute's strings. Plunging head-first toward my watery doom, I leveled my gaze at the twisting form of Natalya. *You'd better know what you're doing,* I thought at Lute. Smoke trailed from my form and carved a sinewy path down the indigo sky.

As I drew level with Natalya, the vapor coalesced around my body and clung to my coat like a cloud of flies on a corpse. It undulated in anticipation until I ripped at the strings, letting a raw boom burst forth from the depths of Lute's souls. The smog around my coat unfurled and snapped outward into streaming, midnight wings. Moonlight shone through them, but they held firm and caught the air like a bat clutching its perch before slumber.

Thunderclap wingbeats pounded with each strum of the strings, and the scream of a murderous falcon belted from my chest and across the night sky. One, two, three massive pumps, and we reached Natalya no more than thirty feet from the lake's surface. She let out a forceful, wheezing grunt as I caught her, oxygen leaving her lungs in a swift but undoubtedly painful exodus.

The added weight of carrying another person dragged us downward until we hovered above the glistening surface, but the glisten was too harsh. Much too harsh for a lake in the summertime.

It was just before our momentum dashed us into the water that I realized the lake was frozen solid. I used the last of my strength to hurl Natalya upward in a desperate attempt to keep her from slamming into the ice.

The same could not be said for me.

While mostly flat and smooth, the surface mercilessly pummeled my frame as I barreled into it. The slick, icy surface pulled at my bloody patches of skin as the moisture met the frigid plane. My grip on Lute jarred loose, and the protective smoke around me dissipated completely. I felt nothing but frosty and indifferent pain until I came to a sliding rest upon the bloody ice. My breath steamed in my eyes, rosy in color as I huffed into a gathering glaze of blood. Metallic sweetness infiltrated my nose with each breath.

An unusually warm stickiness cemented my coat sleeve to my throbbing right arm, and a quick glance toward my extremity revealed my jagged wrist bone protruding from the skin and fabric like a gory middle finger. Ichor gouted from the wound in dwindling spurts. Maybe a bit too brutal. I squeezed my eyes shut and gritted my teeth through biting agony while trying unsuccessfully to sit upright. Blurring vision revealed Natalya lying shivering some ways away from me. Lute rested a short crawl away from her.

"You're going to tell me how you did it," Emile's voice called from beyond my fuzzy line of sight. The bastard must have frozen the surface of the lake before we landed on it. Below us, water pushed persistently upward against the ice. His smooth, condescending words glided across the slick, bloody verglas. "It's near unimaginable what could be accomplished if Shadow Magic were taken seriously as a field of study, as a researched arcana. So you *will* tell me how you controlled it. *Tell me.*" His footsteps squelched in my pooling blood as he approached.

Behind Emile, Natalya stretched out her hands and began hauling herself along the ice toward Lute. One of her legs appeared fractured.

Emile's boot collided with my hip, leaving a bloody sole print against my trousers and shoving me over. "I'd considered that instrument a failed experiment before you brought it back to me. I found the souls—"

"Stole," I wheezed. That earned me a kick to the chest.

"—*Acquired* the souls, and bound them to the instrument, fully knowing that they can't be returned. But what you've done is something I'd very much like to know. You bent the power of the wretches in that block of wood to your will. How depraved and rageful must your soul be to force such a submission? Tell me this instant!" His features were a sickening blend of frustration and academic glee, as if I presented a new challenge to him. I would be his newest study, subjected to horrific and undignified experiments at his cruelly ambitious hand.

Natalya's fingers closed around Lute's neck.

I heaved myself upright and spoke through dribbling blood-spit. "You don't get it, wizard. The souls didn't respond to you because all you value is control. I listen to them, and I feel for them as *equals*. You may have trapped them using shadow magic, but they use their power as they see fit. That's why our Death Metal is stronger than your magic and ambition. Death Metal is about lonely, different, nonconforming, fucked-up souls coming together to share something new, brutal, and beautiful. I'd die for them." As I said it, I realized in my heart that I meant it.

"Oh no, you won't die, bard," he said. "Not until I've extracted the results I require from you." His hands began to blur with a ghostly blue energy. It reflected off the eyes of a corpse that possessed nothing but fiendish desire, truly lifeless and terrifying.

Suddenly, the ice leapt upward, a necrotic bass tone reverberating throughout the solid surface. Fissures spread across the frigid platform in jagged hexes. Emile's feet squeaked and flailed in the slick blood and ice beneath him. I snapped my gaze over to Natalya, who had ripped a dissonant tone from Lute's core. Smog drifted from Lute's vibrating strings, reflecting the faces that Emile had looked in the eye and damned for eternity.

Energy surged through my body as I sprang upward and swung my left arm in a crushing punch. My fist collided with the wizard's face in a solid crunch, a satisfying percussive blow to mirror Natalya's strum. Coat fluttering, Emile hit the crackling ice with a thump followed by the clatter of a couple teeth.

A low grinding approached me as Natalya slung Lute in my direction over the ice. Lute's round wooden body bumped and spun on the splitting support beneath us. The feeling of the red-painted, bloody, cool wood against my hand brought the rushing of thoughts to my mind, both mine and the spirits trapped by Emile. We were a tornado of souls. I couldn't play with my broken arm, not the way I normally did. But no more songwriting would be wasted on the bastard. He didn't deserve it. I raised my good arm above my head just in time to see Emile's eyes widen in genuine fear.

When my left-hand fingers struck the string, my consciousness left me. No longer was I an elf, a musician, or anything tangible. I was the embodiment of vengeance, one of many manifestations of those who were wronged come to rectify the injustice. A massive, explosive hurricane of pitch-black smoke whipped and thrashed around me and Lute, and it grew larger as I tore my fingers across the strings over and over.

The roar of this grainy mass bubbled and dissolved into several distinct voices, all shrieking in unfiltered, molten emotion before reuniting, becoming one chord of death. The fumes tightened and solidified, growing appendages. Claws, eyes, legs, teeth, tongues. They hovered over Emile and drowned out his screams of terror, relishing them. With the force of a dark typhoon, the twisting conglomeration hammered downward and slammed through Emile and the ice with a vile bellow that shook the continent. Frigid lake-water plumed into the air before slapping down onto the now-separating plates of ice.

My shivering hand still ripped at Lute's strings; ferocious claws of a wolverine digging after its prey. Blood dripped from the fingers as they caught the parts of the wire where the gut had worn away. Lute's conjured monstrosity held the dark wizard under, ripping and tearing him apart.

Even in the dark of the night, the water below changed to deep crimson. It was only after the momentum of my last yank of the strings had flung me backward that I stilled, wheezing steam into the unnaturally cool summer air. The remaining wisps of metalsmoke curled above me, casting soothing shapes across the moon before the water slipped over my head. White and black paint curled off my face in the frigid ripples. The cold cradled me gently, guiding me downward toward silence, and even the ringing in my ears faded away. Pins and needles in my fingers and toes from the cold began to give in to numbness, and the light of the moon slowly winked out above me. The relief that Lute and I had done what we set out to do soothed my remaining thoughts. I couldn't even be angry at sharing a watery grave with the bloody chum that used to be Emile.

Performing myself to death was better than I ever could have hoped for.

***

It was the scent of boiled cloth and pungent creams that caused my eyes to flutter, catching glimpses of blurry blues and grays above me. Feeling was still a foreign sensation as I closed them, conserving the strength in my eyelids. Upon opening them again, the hazy vision of a stone ceiling swam into focus as if I were still at the bottom of the lake. My groggy mind stumbled while deciphering the mystery of how that wasn't the case.

In fact, I was lying in a cramped chamber, no more than a couple body lengths wide. The cot I lay on was crisply starched and was perhaps the cleanest bed I'd ever slept on. The royal blue sheet that covered me wasn't quite my color, but judging that I hadn't been awake to object, I elected to ignore it.

A sharp jolt of pain brought my gaze sharply to my right arm, bound snugly in sterile-white plaster and gauze. Several of the more severe cuts and scrapes I had endured during the fight with Emile had been bandaged as well as my head where it had cracked against the Sovereign Stage. One cut had split the new tattoos on my right arm down the middle, and the design refracted where the skin had been stitched back together. I frowned in respect. It looked perfect.

Some time elapsed before the ringing of my ears subsided enough for me to hear the snores of others resting in the infirmary chamber around me. Even my elf's vision had trouble adjusting to the darkness, but I first saw the raven curls dangling in front of a famous bard's face while she slept. A flush of warmth chased away the numbness in my extremities at the sight of Natalya's sleeping form. She sat, straight-backed, in what appeared to be the kingdom's most uncomfortable wooden chair. Her broken leg rested in heavy plaster, but she seemed relatively unhurt otherwise. That was when I noticed the pointed ears of Ord, wedged into the corner with a hand on his knife, ready to defend his charge immediately upon waking.

Ord didn't snore nearly as loudly as Korinne, who leaned against the wall on the opposite side of my cot, Patch's head on her shoulder. The married couple's peaceful expressions contrasted with the angry bruises and bandages they wore, the burns and scratches from fire and ghouls. A pang of guilt flashed through my heart. They'd gotten hurt protecting me and Lute.

*Lute!* I'd forgotten completely about them. My panicked but still not quite adjusted gaze darted around the room until it found a faint shimmer.

"*Mandy*," the voice said, seemingly drained themselves. In the furthest corner of the room, the bloodied, scorched, and battered instrument sat propped against the wall. Outside, I saw the shadowed ponytail of Loukus pacing outside the door, guarding the chamber where we all rested.

Tears choked my next words. "We did it, Lute." They came out as a dry whisper. The battle had likely torched my vocal cords, and my parched throat ached for water or whiskey. Preferably whiskey.

A contented hum reverberated around the room and warmed the space further, the space where my friends slept. "*We did*," they said. We let silence claim the room then, simply basking in the relief that we had made it, that Emile would no longer claim another soul, and that we were together again. As long as I had Lute, I knew I would never truly be alone, and the souls in the instrument would always have someone to fight for them. The world is difficult, and neither of us were cut out for it by ourselves, but we didn't have to be. Through everything, we'd created something powerful and raw, something pitch-black and brutal. And it had revealed a strength neither of us knew we had.

"How do I look?" I asked, suddenly feeling every suture, splint, and dressing.

"Metal."

The End

# ACKNOWLEDGEMENTFEST

## Beta Reader Stage

Calum Lott    Tatiana Obey    ANNIE LAIRD

Isaac Hill    Matt Majewski    Andrew Watson

Kris Marchesi    JONATHAN PUTNAM    Louise Holland

## Technical Stage

**Louise Holland**
T-Swift Expert

**Daly Chochon**
Cover Artist

**Ed cRocKER**
Editor

**Adrian M Gibson**
Stock Images Expert

## Special Thanks Stage

Nick Guerrier    #TheBreakIns

Ryan Leigh    Tatiana Obey

Anthony Schwartz    Scott Leigh

Veronica Leigh    Krista Leigh

Andrew Sutherland    Metalocalypse

Josh Walker    The Reader (You)

The Music

A *note from Rob Leigh*

I've always been a lover of fantastical stories and wrote my own variations on Greek myths at a young age. These stories expanded into inspiration for written works and Tabletop Narratives. During a Tabletop Campaign, I wove a love of music, magic, and heavy metal into a character that would eventually become Mandy. While the campaign eventually came to an end, I decided Mandy's story would not. I wrote this novella as a love letter to all who see music of any genre as a way to connect. There's nothing quite like a music festival to bring people together, and I'd like to think that I put a festival of sorts down in the pages of this book. I hope you enjoyed it!

# Writing Myth & Metal

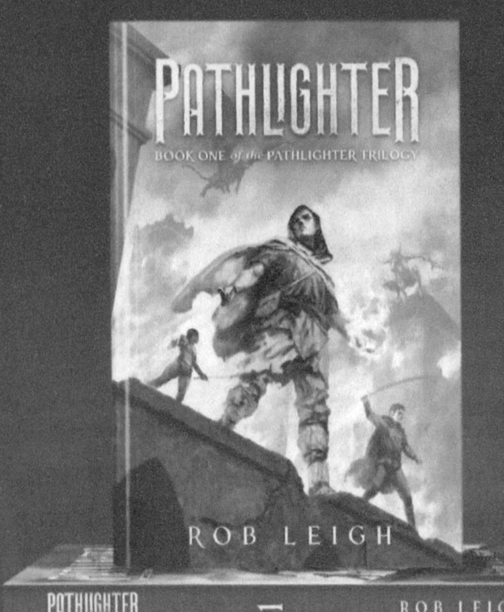

 @robleighauthor

 @problyrobwriter

 www.robleighauthor.com

# Image Attribution & Copyright

**Title Page:** Yurii Zymovin - ID #208903193 - stock.adobe.com (**NOTE:** Original Material has been modified)

**Copyright Page:** tajborg – ID #231755202 – stock.adobe.com (**NOTE:** Original Material has been modified)

**Dedication Page & The End Page:** Nattapol_Sritongcom – ID #289427042 – stock.adobe.com (**NOTE:** Original Material has been modified)

**Performance One:** CROCOTHERY – ID #446433380 – stock.adobe.com (**NOTE:** Original Material has been modified)

**Performance Two:** witoon214 – ID #117572357 – stock.adobe.com (**NOTE:** Original Material has been modified)

**Performance Three:** kucharav – ID #58560937 – stock.adobe.com (**NOTE:** Original Material has been modified)

**Performance Four:** smallredgirl – ID #542361199 – stock.adobe.com (**NOTE:** Original Material has been modified)

**AcknowledgementFest:** Ronny sefria – ID #435609606 – stock.adobe.com (**NOTE:** Original Material has been modified)

**Setlist Page & Also By:** Laura Crazy – ID #23553163 – stock.adobe.com (**NOTE:** Original Material has been modified)

**Filler Page:** Giorgos Karagiannis – ID #245591248 – stock.adobe.com (**NOTE:** Original Material has been modified)